Books in the Replica series

Look out for:

Book 4
Perfect Girls

Marilyn Kaye

Hodder
Children's
Books

a division of Hodder Headline

First published as a Bantam Skylark paperback in the
USA in 1999 by Bantam, Doubleday Dell
Publishing Group Inc, USA

This paperback edition published in Great Britain in 2000
by Hodder Children's Books

10 9 8 7 6 5 4 3 2 1

A Catalogue record for this book
is available from the British Library

ISBN 0340 74954 7

Typeset by Hewer Text Ltd, Edinburgh
Printed and bound in Great Britain by
Clays Ltd, St Ives plc

Hodder Children's Books
A Division of Hodder Headline
338 Euston Road
London NW1 3BH

For my Dutch Treats:
Jeanne-Marie Hilhorst, Marc Langen, and Willem;
Jessie Smits, Theo Van Wijck, and Milou

Memo from the Director

RE: CRESCENT, PHASE II
PREPARATIONS FOR THE NEW YORK GATHERING ARE
UNDER WAY.
EIGHT SUBJECTS ARE CONFIRMED.

1

Amy had the front door open before Tasha could knock. 'I'm leaving, Mom,' she called. 'Tasha's here!'

Her mother's usual parting words followed her out the door: 'Have a good day, girls!'

Tasha was waiting on the steps. She frowned. 'I heard that,' she said. 'Can you tell me one *good* thing about Mondays?'

Amy had to think about that. As the two of them walked out of the apartment block where they lived next door to each other, she said, 'Mondays are good because – because we're having another Awareness Assembly fifth period.'

Tasha brightened. 'That's right. No P.E for me. What about you?'

'English. Just my luck, I miss my favourite class. If only I'd known they were going to have these assemblies Monday this month, I would have asked for geography fifth period.' She stopped walking suddenly. 'I hear Eric.'

Tasha uttered a mild groan. 'Do you hear him coming out the door or getting out of bed? Because *I'm* not waiting forever.'

Amy laughed. 'I wouldn't know if he was just getting out of bed, Tasha. My ears aren't *that* good.'

'Exactly how *well* can you hear?' Tasha asked. 'Like, when I'm on the phone in my room, can you hear me in your room?'

'You're becoming paranoid,' Amy said. She smiled mischievously. 'Unless you're saying things you don't want me to hear.'

'No. I'm just curious,' Tasha said. 'Can you hear through walls?'

'Sometimes,' Amy admitted. 'It depends on how thick the wall is, and how loud the noise is. And I have to be tuned in, you know? I need to be listening for something I want to hear.'

'So *that's* why you always know when my brother is around,' Tasha said.

'Shhh!' Amy hissed. Eric didn't have Amy's acute

hearing, but he wasn't deaf. And he was right behind them now.

But Eric hadn't heard his sister. He had other things on his mind when he caught up with the girls. 'Are we having another one of those Learn Something assemblies today?'

'It's called an Awareness Assembly,' Tasha corrected him. 'Yeah, fifth period.'

Eric let out a massive sigh of relief. 'No Spanish.'

'I thought you liked Spanish,' Amy commented.

'It's okay. But I forgot to do the homework assignment.'

Amy and Tasha exchanged looks. Eric's problem with memory was well known. It was something Amy had difficulty understanding. 'How can you forget about homework? Don't you write down the assignment?'

'Sure, but sometimes I forget to look at what I write down. Hey, not all of us are perfect, you know.'

Tasha gave him a disdainful look. 'Eric, *I* remember to check my homework assignments every day, and I'm not perfect.'

Eric nodded. 'You can say that again. Hey, Amy, any chance you could give Tasha a little of your superior genetic material?'

'Oh, shut up,' Amy said good-naturedly. It wasn't long ago that Amy had discovered the truth about her birth – that she had been created by scientists working on Project Crescent, a government experiment so highly classified that no official knowledge of it existed. The scientists recruited to work on the project had collected and manipulated the best in human genetics – and the result had been Amy. Actually, twelve Amys. All identical. All clones. Unearthing the truth had been an incredible shock for Amy, but she'd finally accepted it, and had recently shared her secret with Eric and Tasha. It used to bother her when one of them commented on her special nature. Now she was accustomed to Eric's teasing, and it didn't matter – as long as the wrong people didn't hear about it. She changed the subject. 'Why do they call it an 'awareness' assembly, anyway?'

'I guess because they're supposed to make us aware of some problem we don't usually think about,' Tasha said. 'Like that first one on recycling. I had no idea that plastic bottles can last practically forever.'

'Last week's was pretty good, too,' Amy noted.

Eric scratched his head. 'Which one was that?'

'How deaf people get along. Remember, that lady showed us how she uses sign language and reads lips?' Amy grinned. 'Didn't you love it when she saw Jeanine tell someone the assembly was boring? And the interpreter said it out loud? I thought Jeanine was going to die.'

'Unfortunately, she's alive and well,' Tasha commented.

'Tasha, don't talk like that! I don't like Jeanine, but I don't wish her *dead*.'

Tasha shrugged. 'Why not? I'll be that's how she'd like to see *you*. You two have been sworn enemies since first grade.'

'That's just because we're always competing with each other,' Amy said. 'Spelling bees, gymnastics, everything.'

'But now you have an unfair advantage,' Tasha said. 'Jeanine didn't have a bunch of scientists working on her when she was born. Though I've always thought she might have had a personality transplant. From Dr Jekyll.'

'I don't think we really *hate* each other,' Amy noted. 'At least, not enough to commit murder.'

'What are you competing for now?' Eric asked.

'Nothing, really,' Amy said. 'Just the usual. Grades. Shoes.'

'What about the essay contest?' Tasha remarked.

Amy nodded. 'I almost forgot about that. Ms Weller invited a bunch of her English students to enter the National Essay Competition,' she explained to Eric. 'We were given a topic and had to write an essay in one hour, without any preparation.'

'When do you find out who won?' Eric asked.

'I don't know. All the essays were sent off to some national office, where they pick the semi-finalists. The topic was pretty interesting, actually: peer pressure. I wrote about how cliques form and how people knock themselves out trying to get in without even knowing why.'

'Jeanine may have the unfair advantage there,' said Tasha. 'I mean, *look* at her.'

They'd reached Parkside Middle School, and Jeanine Bryant could be seen with some other students sitting on the steps leading to the entrance.

'Ever since Jeanine started hanging out with that crowd, she's been imitating them,' Tasha continued. 'Did you notice how she put a red streak in her hair last week? All the girls in that crowd have red streaks.'

'Who's in that crowd, anyway?' Amy asked, looking at the half dozen kids sprawled on the steps. 'I don't know any of them.'

Tasha was always more tuned in to school gossip. 'They're mostly eighth- and ninth-graders,' she replied. Both girls looked at Eric. As a ninth grader, he was now expected to provide them with information.

But Eric wasn't exactly the most social guy in his class. 'I don't know,' he said vaguely. 'They're not jocks, or stoners, or punks. I think they're just another popular crowd.'

As they climbed the steps, Jeanine raised her voice. 'That party Saturday night was great!' she said. 'All the really cool kids were there. And *so* select.' Amy rolled her eyes. It was obvious that Jeanine wanted to be overheard. Given their on-going rivalry, Amy didn't doubt that Jeanine probably thought that she, Amy, was jealous of Jeanine's newfound popularity. If that was true, Jeanine couldn't be more wrong. No way was Amy jealous. And she didn't care if Jeanine was in a clique and she wasn't. That notion didn't appeal to Amy at all. She liked having only a couple of really close friends. With her secret, she couldn't let just anyone into her private world.

But Amy wasn't beyond wanting to beat Jeanine in that essay competition . . .

The friends separated to go to their homerooms. Tasha and Amy decided on a place to meet fifth period so they could go to the assembly together. Eric didn't offer to join them, and they didn't invite him. There was an unwritten law at Parkside about seating arrangements − in the cafeteria, the gym, anywhere the entire school congregated. It didn't matter that Eric was now Amy's sort-of official boyfriend. He was in the ninth grade, she was in the seventh grade, and any real socialising had to take place off campus.

So when Amy entered the gym with Tasha fifth period, she knew Eric was somewhere high on the bleachers with track team and basketball buddies from his grade. Eighth-graders got the lower levels of the bleachers and the back rows of the folding chairs set up on the gym floor. She and Tasha proceeded to the front of the gym, where seventh-graders were taking seats. The area was filled with the cries of 'Lisa, over here,' and 'Sorry, this seat's saved.'

'Honestly,' Tasha remarked, 'you'd think these girls would collapse if they had to spend one hour sitting next to someone other than their best friend.'

'I know,' Amy said as she sat down beside her. 'Everyone's so gutless.' She looked around, curious to see if Jeanine had the guts to abandon the unofficial seventh-grade area so she could sit with her older friends. But no, traditions were too strong. Jeanine was sitting way over on the other side of the first row, with her regular friend Linda Riviera.

Amy was about to point this out to Tasha, when she noticed that Tasha was scratching her wrist under her bracelet. 'If it itches you, why don't you take it off?' said Amy.

'Because it looks too gross,' Tasha told her. She undid the clasp on the silver cuff. 'See?'

'Yuck.' It did look pretty gross – tiny, fiery red spots covered the skin that had been concealed by the bracelet. 'How did that happen?'

'It's a skin allergy,' Tasha said. 'I'm allergic to nickel.'

'But you wear that bracelet all the time. How come it just started bothering you?' Amy peered at the wide cuff bracelet. 'Isn't it silver?'

'It's only plated in silver, and the silver's wearing

off. Look.' Tasha showed Amy the inside of the bracelet, where a dark smudge had formed. 'That must be nickel underneath,' she added as she started to put the bracelet back on.

'You're not going to wear it, are you?'

'But I feel naked without it,' Tasha said mournfully. 'You're not allergic to anything, are you?'

'I kind of doubt it,' Amy admitted. That was the great advantage to being a genetically perfect clone. She was never sick. She didn't get hay fever, she could eat anything, and she could wear any kind of jewellery. She didn't wear much, though. Just her watch and the pearl ring her mother had given her when she turned twelve. And her pendant, of course.

Automatically, her hand went to the thin silver chain, and she felt the curve of the small crescent moon that dangled from it. She had been given this pendant by a very special person, Dr Jaleski, who had been the director of Project Crescent. He was dead now, and his daughter had told Amy he'd made this pendant for her so she'd never forget who she was. It was certainly easier to look at the sterling silver crescent than to try to get a look at the identical shape, a birthmark, on her right shoulder blade.

Their principal, Dr Noble, was tapping on the microphone. 'Could I have your attention, please? Thank you. Welcome to our Awareness Assembly. Today we are going to address a very serious topic. There is a plague among us, a disease which threatens to wipe out your entire generation. It is a ruthless killer that has infiltrated our society and selected adolescents as its main victims.'

Everyone was on the edge of their seats. Tasha had even stopped scratching her arm.

'I am speaking, of course, about . . . drug abuse.'

People let out a few groans and relaxed their bodies. From the way Dr Noble had been talking, they had been expecting some amazing and exciting new horror. But this was old news. Everyone knew how bad drugs were, they'd been told about the dangers practically since they were babies, and drugs weren't a particularly big problem at Parkside anyway.

This assembly didn't look like it would be telling them anything they didn't already know. For the next thirty minutes, a doctor talked about the health risks; a police officer talked about criminal consequences; and a drug counsellor talked about getting help if you were already on drugs. Everything they said was true, but everyone in the gym had heard it all before.

There was a mild flutter of interest when the last speaker was introduced. 'That guy looks familiar,' Amy commented.

'He's an actor. He was on that soap we used to watch,' Tasha told her. 'He drowned. No, wait, he fell off a mountain. Something like that. Anyway, he disappeared and I haven't seen him on TV since then. I always wondered what happened to him.'

Apparently, he had become a drug addict. He told them how he started taking drugs so he could stay up all night and party and still make it to the soap opera's set early in the morning. 'I was making a lot of money back then, but it all went on drugs. And eventually it started to affect my work on the soap opera. I was fired. I got so depressed, I did more drugs. And when those drugs couldn't do it for me any more, I tried something new.'

This new drug turned out to be the worst yet. 'It's got several street names, but the most popular one is 'Toast', the actor told them. 'People say it's called that because it smells like cinnamon toast. I say it got that name because once you start on it, you're toast.' He explained how Toast cost him his career, his girlfriend, and his home; he ended up in hospital, almost dead. Then he got into a recovery programme, and now he was clean and sober. The only time the audience listened with real interest was when he described the bad effects of the drug.

'You sweat, your stomach goes berserk, you puke your guts out, and you pull your own hair out of your head.'

When he finished, there was polite applause and then a general shuffling sound as kids began gathering their things. 'Are you more aware now?' Tasha asked Amy.

'Not really,' Amy replied. 'I just don't think I'll ever be able to eat cinnamon toast again.' She reached for her backpack.

But the assembly wasn't over. Dr Noble was at the microphone again. 'Before you go on to your sixth-period classes, we have an announcement to make. Ms Weller will tell you about it.'

'Maybe this is about the essay competition,' Amy murmured. She glanced over at Jeanine, who was clearly having the same thought. She was telling Linda, 'She's going to announce the winner of the essay contest.'

Did Jeanine know that or was she just guessing?

Amy wondered. Then it dawned on her that there was no way she could have heard Jeanine from this distance, not even with her skills. 'Hey, I think I know how to lip-read now,' Amy whispered to Tasha. Tasha wasn't surprised. She knew all about Amy's ability to see something once and imitate it perfectly.

Ms Weller came up to the microphone. 'I'm very pleased to announce that not one, but *two* Parkside students have been selected as finalists in the National Essay Competition! These two seventh-graders will have an all-expenses-paid trip to New York City to compete in the finals. Congratulations to Jeanine Bryant and Amy Candler!'

Tasha let out a whoop as the audience applauded. Amy could feel Jeanine's eyes on her, but her superior abilities didn't include knowing what the girl was thinking. Was Jeanine furious that she had to share this honour? Personally, Amy didn't care at all. She was more excited at the thought of going to New York.

There was something else she had to think about too, and Tasha voiced the concern for her. 'What's your mother going to say?' she asked as they filed out of the gymnasium. 'You know she doesn't like you to call attention to yourself.'

'She doesn't want me to be an Olympic gymnast and get my face on a cereal box. But this is different,' Amy reasoned. 'Winning an essay contest doesn't make a person famous.'

Still, she had a feeling that her mother wasn't going to be too thrilled. She didn't like Amy to compete in sports or academics or anything. Because Amy always excelled. And people were going to start wondering why.

2

Nancy Candler's reaction to the news came as no surprise to Amy, and Tasha had been correct. Nancy was not pleased.

'Oh, Amy,' Nancy said as she sank down into a chair at the kitchen table.

Amy knew what was coming and tried to ward it off. 'Gee, Mom, aren't you proud of me? Any ordinary mother would be saying congratulations.'

'Any ordinary mother of an ordinary child,' Nancy corrected her. She shook her head reprovingly. 'How many times have I told you—'

'I know, I know,' Amy interrupted. 'I'm not supposed to call attention to myself. I shouldn't stand out in the crowd and I shouldn't be noticed.'

'It's for your own good, Amy. There are people out there who want to find you.'

'They've already found me, Mom.'

Her mother couldn't argue with that. Too many incidents, too many close calls had made it clear to them that Amy had been identified. They knew now that the faceless organisation, the powers behind Project Crescent, had never bought the story that all twelve clones had been destroyed in the explosion of the laboratory twelve years ago. An explosion deliberately set off by Dr Jaleski and several other scientists, including Amy's mother. They had stumbled on the real reason they were creating clones, which wasn't to benefit human-kind, but to create a superior race. The clones, with every facet of their human potential maximised, would enable the faceless organisation to achieve world dominance. The explosion was staged to seem like an accident, and the babies were reported to have perished in the ensuing blaze. But the babies had been whisked away and sent far and wide for adoption. Nancy Candler had kept Amy – Amy, Number Seven. The other Amys were alive and out there, somewhere. Amy herself had identified two others – a French ballerina and an actress. What the organisation wanted from the clones now wasn't completely clear, and Amy wasn't sure she wanted to know.

She did know that her mother wanted to protect her, and so far she'd tried to follow Nancy's advice. She kept a low profile and didn't exhibit her extraordinary gifts – well, not publicly. She'd given up gymnastics, she held herself back in sports and let others win the races, and only occasionally did she allow herself to be the first with a hand up in class. She knew she couldn't let the whole world see how exceptional she was. It wasn't easy for a person who was naturally competitive.

But this was different. 'This has nothing to do with my, you know, abilities, Mom. I had to be creative when I wrote the essay, not just smart. And I wasn't *that* exceptional. I'm not the only finalist at Parkside.'

Her mother's eyebrows went up. 'You're not?'

'Jeanine Bryant was picked too.' Amy'd never thought she'd be happy to find herself associated with Jeanine, but if this fact got her to the nationals, she didn't mind at all. And it did look like the disapproval in Nancy's eyes was easing up a little.

She pressed her advantage, continuing, 'Besides,

no one pays attention to something like an essay contest. Nobody cares. It isn't like the National Spelling Bee, where the winners are on TV.' She rummaged through her backpack and pulled out a brochure. 'Ms Weller told me to give this to you. It explains the whole competition. There's a permission sheet for you to sign.'

Nancy sighed, but she took the brochure and began to scan the pages. Then she looked up. 'New York? The finals are in New York?'

'Didn't I mention that?' Amy asked innocently. A slight smile tickled her mother's lips. 'No, dear, you didn't.'

'It's all expenses paid for the contestant and a parent,' Amy pointed out quickly. 'We'd fly to New York and stay at a fancy hotel, all for free! And we get a tour of the city, and a boat ride, and tickets to a real Broadway play! Mom, I've never been to New York!'

'Amy, you're only twelve years old,' her mother said dryly. 'When I was your age, I hadn't been to New York, either.'

'But we can't pass up a chance like this! Just think about it, Mom! The Statue of Liberty, and China-town, and shopping . . . and of course, lots of great educational opportunities,' she added hastily. 'Museums and all that stuff. And Mom, I promise, I *swear*, I'll do my best not to win.' She meant that, too. She wouldn't really mind all that much if she lost to another finalist – as long as that finalist wasn't Jeanine.

Nancy was weakening, she could see that. At least, now she was reading the material with more attention.

Then Nancy frowned. 'The week of the eighteenth . . .'

'It's spring break. I wouldn't even miss any school.'

Now Nancy was shaking her head, and she really looked regretful. 'That's the week of my conference, honey. I told you about that.'

For someone with a superior memory, Amy had somehow managed to let that piece of information slip out of her head. 'The one in Africa?' she asked in dismay.

Nancy nodded. 'I'm sorry, Amy. It's a very important meeting, and I'm committed. I'm giving a paper on molecular biology, remember?'

How could she have forgotten? Her mother had been working long hours at the university laboratory doing the research for this paper.

Amy made a half-hearted attempt to propose an option. 'You don't have to go with me,' she began, but she knew this was out of the question. There was no way her mother would let her go off to New York alone.

Nancy was truly regretful. She took Amy's hand. 'Does the competition mean that much to you?'

It was a disappointment, but Amy didn't want to make her mother feel worse than she already did. 'I was more excited about going to New York,' she admitted. But in the back of her mind, she could see Jeanine's happy face when she learned Amy wouldn't be competing. It wasn't a pretty sight.

Nancy squeezed her hand. 'I'll make it up to you, sweetie. Maybe we can take a vacation in New York this summer. How would you like that?'

'Sounds great,' Amy said, forcing a smile. She retrieved the brochure and the unsigned permission sheet and stuck them in her backpack. Then she looked at the clock. 'I guess we should start getting dinner together, huh?'

They were having guests that evening – the whole Morgan family was coming over for dinner. Amy had planned to make a special dessert, a chocolate-chip pie with caramel sauce, with Eric in mind. She threw herself into the job, taking out her frustrations as she mixed the pie filling.

As she worked, she realised that her mother hadn't said anything about what Amy would be doing while she was away at her conference. Nancy wouldn't leave her home alone any sooner than she'd let her go off to New York by herself. Amy just hoped her 'babysitter' would be Monica Jackson, a neighbour and former college classmate of Nancy's, and not some person hired from an agency. Unfortunately, as much as Nancy liked Monica, she thought the flamboyant artist was a little irresponsible.

Actually, Amy supposed she could use the situation to her advantage. Her mother had to be feeling pretty guilty about depriving her of a trip to New York, so Amy could probably get her way about Monica. This might also be a good time to butter Nancy up for some clothes, maybe those platform sandals she'd seen at the mall . . .

Tasha, Eric, and their parents arrived promptly at seven. As Nancy served drinks, Amy ordered Tasha and Eric back to the kitchen to help her set the table. There she told them the bad news about New York.

'I *told* you she wouldn't let you go,' Tasha said, but at least she had the courtesy to look sympathetic.

Eric expressed himself in his usual succinct way. 'That sucks.'

'Well, look on the bright side,' Tasha suggested.

'What bright side?'

'*I'll* be here. We can hang out.'

Considering the fact that she and Tasha were always hanging out, that wasn't an exciting prospect, but Amy nodded. 'If it's warm enough, maybe we can go to the beach.'

'I'll be here too,' Eric said unexpectedly.

Both Amy and Tasha looked at him in surprise. 'What about your camping trip?'

'Kyle's been grounded for bad grades. And camping alone is definitely no fun.'

'As if Mom would let you go alone anyway,' Tasha pointed out.

Eric ignored his sister's comment. 'So maybe we could do stuff,' he said to Amy. 'Like bowling. I wonder if you could score a perfect game.'

'I could *try*,' she said.

'Cool,' he replied.

Their gazes locked. Tasha let out her standard

groan and picked up the stack of dishes. 'Don't miss me too much,' she said as she left the kitchen and went into the dining-room.

For the first time since she came home from school, Amy was able to smile without effort. She was so lucky with Eric. Some other guy, *any* other guy, might not like knowing his girlfriend could do just about anything better than he could. But Eric had been impressed with Amy's skills even before he knew that she was a clone. And when she had revealed the truth about herself, he hadn't been grossed out. He'd been even more impressed.

He gave a quick look over his shoulder to make sure Tasha wasn't coming. Then he moved in closer and gave Amy a brief kiss.

They parted just in time. Tasha was hurrying back into the kitchen. She looked excited. 'I know a secret,' she sang out.

'What?' Amy asked.

'You're going to stay with us while your mother's in Africa.'

Amy's eyes lit up. 'Really?' She hadn't held any hope for this possibility. She'd stayed with the Morgans just a month ago, when her mother had been hospitalised, so she'd been sure her mother wouldn't ask them to take her again.

'I heard them talking in the living room. Your mother was saying no, no, she couldn't impose and all that, but my mother insisted.'

'Cool!' Eric declared.

Tasha gave him a look. 'She'll be staying in *my* room.' She turned to Amy. 'Act surprised when they tell you.'

Amy did just that over dessert, when she heard the news officially. 'Mom, that's great!' she squealed. 'Thanks, Mrs Morgan, Mr Morgan. I won't be any trouble, I promise.'

Nancy smiled. 'I hope this helps make up for the contest.'

'What contest?' Mrs Morgan asked.

'I told you, Mom, Amy won an essay competition,' Tasha said.

'I didn't win anything,' Amy corrected her. 'I'm a finalist. But I can't go to the national competition because it's in New York over the spring break.'

Mr Morgan's face went all dreamy at the mention of New York. 'My favourite city in the world,' he said. 'The last time we were there, I went to every jazz club in Greenwich Village.'

25

'What do you mean, "the last time we were there"?' Eric questioned. *'We've* never been to New York.'

'I meant your mother and me,' Mr Morgan told him. 'We had a life before you kids were born, you know.'

'It's been fifteen years since we've seen the New York skyline,' Mrs Morgan mused. 'We stayed at a lovely hotel, right on Central Park, and we went to the theatre almost every night. And the restaurants! Unbelievable.' She looked at her husband. 'Remember the horse-drawn carriage ride we took through the park? It was so romantic.' She smiled at Nancy. 'Eric was born nine months later.'

Eric scrunched his face in agony. *'Mom.'*

'We need to get back there one of these days,' Mr Morgan said. 'Show the kids the sights, take in some theatre . . .'

'See the Knicks play,' Eric said.

'Tasha, why are you rubbing your wrist like that?' Mrs Morgan asked.

'Huh? Oh. I broke out from my bracelet. I guess it has nickel in it.'

'Nickel allergies are very common,' Nancy remarked. 'If you really love your bracelet, just paint the inside with clear nail polish. Your rash will disappear.'

'Okay,' Tasha said. Then her eyes widened. 'How about over spring break?'

Her mother looked at her blankly. 'What?'

'Let's go to New York over spring break!' Tasha's voice rose an octave, as it always did when she had a brilliant idea. 'Really, think about it, this would be perfect! Amy could come with us, and then she could be in the essay final!'

'Now, Tasha,' Nancy remonstrated.

Mrs Morgan, however, was looking at her daughter thoughtfully. 'You know, that's not such a crazy idea.'

'Are you serious?' Mr Morgan said, looking at her in disbelief. 'Spring break is just next month, isn't it?'

'Two weeks from now,' Eric told him.

'We can't just drop everything and go to New York in two weeks!' his father declared.

'Of course not,' Nancy said quickly. 'Tasha, it's sweet of you to think about Amy, but—'

'No, wait,' Mrs Morgan interrupted excitedly. 'Why not? We don't have anything else planned. I could arrange the whole trip with a travel agent tomorrow. There are some excellent airfares. I saw an ad in yesterday's paper.' She turned to her husband. 'And *you* need a vacation.'

'So do I,' Eric added quickly.

His father snorted. 'Your life is one long vacation.'

'Daddy, it would be so fabulous,' Tasha shrieked. '*Please?*'

Amy hid her smile. Tasha only called her father Daddy when she really wanted something. But she had to admit, she was getting pretty excited herself at the prospect. 'And one of you could go for free,' she told them. 'It says in the brochure, free airfare for a parent or guardian!'

'The Knicks, Dad,' Eric added. 'The Knicks!'

'Remember the pastrami at the Carnegie Deli?' Mrs Morgan wheedled.

Mr Morgan was beginning to look tempted. Amy could see it written all over his face. 'Well . . .'

'No, this is crazy,' Nancy protested. 'I can't ask you to take Amy to New York!'

'You're not asking us,' Mrs Morgan said briskly. 'We're inviting her.' She nudged her husband. 'Aren't we?'

He gave in. 'Why not?'

Tasha and Eric began to make whooping sounds. Amy looked at her mother anxiously. 'Mom . . . ?'

Nancy looked torn. Then she uttered another of her resigned sighs and smiled. 'Get the permission sheet.'

3

'I n a few moments we will begin our descent into New York City's John F. Kennedy Airport. Passengers should return to their seats and fasten their seat belts. Please also return your seats and tray tables to their upright positions.'

Amy listened to the in-flight announcement and fiddled with the lever by her seat. The back pulled up. She handed her soda can to the passing flight attendant, took off her headset, and checked to make sure her seat belt was still buckled. Then she strained to get a look out of the window at the New York skyline. They were still too high, and it was probably too cloudy anyway. It didn't matter; she was content. The flight from Los Angeles had been smooth, the food had been pretty good, and they'd been shown a funny movie. Everything was perfect.

Well, almost perfect.

She poked Eric, and he opened his eyes. 'Are we there?' he asked.

'Almost,' Amy said. 'You have to pull your seat up now.'

She looked to her other side. Tasha was still engrossed in her tourist guide. 'Listen, it says here that the ancestors of one out of every two people came to this country through Ellis Island. There's even a museum. We have to see it.' She scribbled in her little notebook, adding Ellis Island to the growing list of places to visit.

Amy looked at the list. 'We're only going to be in New York for a week, Tasha,' she reminded her friend. 'And some of that time I'll be busy doing essay stuff. There's a get-together for the contestants tomorrow morning, then the actual competition on Tuesday. They announce the winner at the banquet on Thursday.'

'That leaves plenty of time to see everything,' Tasha assured her. 'All the museums, of course. Plus we've got tickets to *Cats* on Monday, and we're going to Rockefeller Center to see if we can get into a TV show.'

'Knicks on Wednesday,' Eric reminded her.

Tasha wrote that down. 'Too bad this isn't December. There's always a huge Christmas tree at Rockefeller Center, and ice skating . . .' Her voice trailed off as she consulted her guidebook.

Eric spoke in a low voice. 'You know, we don't have to do *everything* on her list.'

'You have other ideas?' Amy asked him.

'Well, I was thinking . . . maybe we could take one of those horse-drawn carriage rides my mother was talking about. Just you and me.'

'Really?' Amy was more than pleased. 'That would be great.'

'What are you two whispering about?' chirped a voice from the aisle.

Amy's smile faded. 'You're supposed to be in your seat, Jeanine.'

'I'm on my way,' Jeanine sang out. 'See you in New York!'

Eric watched Jeanine prance back to her seat and wrinkled his nose. 'She's not going to do everything with us, is she?'

'I don't know,' Amy said mournfully. 'I hope not, but your mother might insist that we take her around.'

'Maybe we could dump her on Tasha.'

'I couldn't do that to my best friend,' Amy reprimanded him. But she understood how Eric felt. It had been a blow when they'd learned that Jeanine would be a part of their contingent. Her parents couldn't come to New York with her, and because Mrs Morgan took Jeanine to gymnastics with Tasha it was easy for Mrs Bryant to call and ask if they'd be able to take Jeanine to New York with them.

Amy sincerely doubted that Jeanine wanted to hang out with them, either. No, she amended that. Jeanine would probably love to get some time alone with Eric. And although Amy knew that Eric had no interest in Jeanine, she didn't particularly want to give Jeanine any opportunities to change his mind about her.

As the plane began its descent, it occurred to Amy that with her physical strength, she could easily put Jeanine out of the picture. Not that she would ever seriously hurt Jeanine, but a simple handshake could lead to some broken bones for the nasty girl. Which would have the added benefit of making her unable to write an essay.

Amy wasn't thinking seriously, of course. But even so . . . it was lucky for Jeanine that Amy had morals.

4

T asha had never stayed in a hotel room this nice before. It wasn't just a room — it was a suite, two bedrooms connected by a living-room. At the window, she looked out onto the New York street from twenty storeys above. Then she checked her tourist guide.

'Did you know,' she said, 'that there are twelve thousand yellow taxicabs on the streets of New York?'

There was no response. Tasha liked learning interesting little facts, but no one was listening. Her mother was directing the bellboy who had brought up the suitcases. Her father was studying the contents of the mini-bar. Eric was examining the card on the TV that listed the movie channels available. And Amy was engrossed in reading the material from the National Essay Competition that had been given to her when they checked in.

Tasha went back to her guide. 'Did you know that there are a hundred and twenty museums in New York? We're here for seven days; that makes . . .' She tried to do some mental maths.

Amy responded. 'Approximately seventeen point one four three museums per day.'

Eric looked at her in alarm. 'No way I'm going to a hundred and twenty museums,' he declared.

'No, I guess we'll have to pick and choose,' Tasha said.

'Tasha, you and Amy will take the room with the two single beds,' Mrs Morgan announced. 'Your father and I will take the other bedroom.'

'What about me?' Eric asked.

'You'll be in here,' she told him. 'This sofa pulls out into a bed.'

'Whew, that's a relief,' Eric commented. 'For a minute I thought you were going to tell me I had to share a room with Jeanine.'

Tasha and Amy began to laugh, but Mrs Morgan shot him a withering look. 'Don't talk nonsense. Jeanine has her own room right across the hall.'

Now Tasha and Amy breathed sighs of relief. Tasha had been afraid that the three girls might have to share a bedroom. But she should have guessed that Jeanine's wealthy parents would provide her with a room of her very own.

'Are all the essay contestants staying at this hotel, Amy?' Mrs Morgan asked her.

Amy was still going over the official information. 'That's what it says here. We're all supposed to meet at dinner tonight, and we can bring our families. That means you guys can all come.' She looked at the schedule again. 'It's the Blue Room on the twenty-second floor. Wow, it says here there are a hundred and fifteen kids in this competition.'

'Are you sure this dinner isn't just for the competition participants?' Mr Morgan asked.

'Nope, it says right here, all family members accompanying the participants are invited to join. And you guys are my family this week.'

'And Jeanine's family,' Mrs Morgan reminded her. As soon as her back was turned, Tasha and Amy automatically made silent gagging motions.

'A hundred and fifteen contestants plus families,' Mr Morgan mused. 'I hope it's a big room.'

It was. The Blue Room turned out to be a

ballroom, very fancy, with elaborate chandeliers hanging from high ceilings. At least fifty round tables filled the space, all beautifully set with flowers and white linen. A card bearing a number stood in each floral centrepiece. At one end of the room was a long table, above which hung a banner that read WELCOME NATIONAL ESSAY FINALISTS.

'Do I look okay?' Amy asked Tasha anxiously.

'Perfect,' Tasha assured her. They hadn't been sure how people would dress for this dinner, but they wanted to save their best outfits for the awards banquet, so they were wearing their second-best outfits. For Amy, that was a long flowered skirt with a pink silk T-shirt. Looking at the other kids wandering around the ballroom, Tasha decided Amy fitted in just fine. She did too, with her pale green shift dress and matching cardigan.

Jeanine, naturally, outshone them both – at least, in her own mind, Tasha believed. She wore a very short black dress made out of shiny material that gleamed under the chandeliers. Tasha had noticed how her mother had pursed her lips in disapproval when Jeanine had appeared at the door of their suite, but since Jeanine wasn't *her* daughter, Mrs Morgan hadn't said anything. Tasha wouldn't have been allowed out of her room wearing a dress like that. Personally, she thought it was much too dressy.

Amy apparently thought so too. 'Jeanine, where did you get that dress?' she asked.

'Oh, you wouldn't know this store, Amy,' Jeanine said, giving her a condescending smile. 'It's over in Beverly Hills.' She smoothed her skirt. 'The salesgirl said it gave me real New York attitude.'

'And what's that?' Tasha inquired.

The snotty smile remained firmly in place. 'That's not easy to explain. It has to do with, you know, being sophisticated. Acting bored, like you've seen everything before.' Jeanine strolled away from their group and disappeared in the crowd.

'Where is she going?' Amy whispered to Tasha.

'Who knows, who cares?' Tasha replied. 'She probably thinks she's too sophisticated to be seen with us.'

Amy nodded fervently. 'I can't believe she wants to look bored. What's cool about that?'

'Nothing,' Tasha said. 'She isn't pulling it off anyway. I've never seen her more excited.'

A beaming man wearing a badge approached

them. 'Good evening! I'm George Drexel, co-chairman of the National Essay Competition.' He shook hands with the Morgan parents, who introduced themselves, Eric, and the girls. Mr Drexel shook hands with them, too, but he held on to Amy's a little longer. 'Congratulations on making it this far, young lady,' he told her. 'And good luck! Now, if you'll go over to that table under the banner, you'll find a name tag for yourself, and a number indicating what table you and your guests have been assigned.'

Amy turned to Tasha. 'Come with me?'

'Okay.'

Eric, who was looking distinctly uncomfortable in his jacket and tie, remained with his parents while Amy and Tasha went to the table. They waited as a smiling woman spoke to another contestant and located her tag.

Jeanine was there, too, talking animatedly with a girl whose name tag read SARAH MILLER, NORMAN, OKLAHOMA. The tag was useful, since Jeanine didn't bother to make introductions. But as Amy collected her own name tag, Jeanine actually spoke to them.

'I'm learning about the best places to shop in New York,' she told them. 'There's an area called

SoHo that's supposed to be awesome, right?' She turned to the Oklahoma girl for confirmation.

'It's the trendiest part of New York,' Sarah Miller confirmed. 'I'm going there tomorrow afternoon. You want to come?'

'Absolutely!' Jeanine declared. Sarah turned to Amy and Tasha.

'How about you guys?'

'No, thanks,' Tasha said. 'I'm going to the Museum of Modern Art tomorrow.'

Jeanine brushed that notion away. 'Oh, that's a waste of time. You can see plenty of modern art in Los Angeles.' She looked at Amy. 'Amy, wouldn't you rather come shopping with us?'

'No thanks,' Amy said. She tugged at Tasha's arm, and they started back towards where they'd left the Morgans.

'I can't believe Jeanine asked us to go,' Tasha said.

Amy shrugged. 'Maybe she was trying to impress Sarah with what a nice person she is.'

'She's a pretty good actress,' Tasha commented. 'She sounded like she actually *wanted* you to come with them.'

Amy grinned. 'Probably because she was sure I'd say no. She knows I'd rather spend my time with

41

you. Even if that *does* mean going to a hundred and twenty museums.'

'Okay, okay,' Tasha said, relenting. 'We can go shopping, too.' She looked back at Jeanine. 'I hope she gets to be real buddy-buddy with that girl Sarah. Then maybe we won't see her all week. Hey, if we're really lucky, maybe she'll even want to eat dinner with her.'

But the tables were assigned, so Jeanine was with them. She was still acting happy and excited, too. She was sitting next to Eric, which was probably improving for her mood.

Jeanine never gave up, Tasha mused. She'd been coming on to Eric for over a month now. Eric hadn't given her any encouragement, but even so, Jeanine never missed a chance to flirt. She probably couldn't accept the fact that a boy existed on the face of the earth who wasn't interested in her.

Thank goodness Eric was immune to her charms. Tasha could remember how shocked – no, *horrified* – she'd been when Jeanine first started asking her about Eric, talking about how cute he was and whether he had a girlfriend. Then Tasha reminded herself that she hadn't been too thrilled when she realised Amy had a romantic interest in Eric, too.

That was different, though. Amy was her best friend; they'd been best friends forever. Other friends said 'AmyandTasha' as if they were one person, and Eric had never been part of the equation before. When they were younger, he had been the enemy, or someone they just ignored. But they were growing up, and the battles they'd fought in the past were kids' stuff.

Tasha glanced at Amy, sitting on Eric's other side. The first course, a creamy soup, was being served, but Amy didn't even notice. She was busy looking into Eric's eyes, listening to whatever he was saying. Amazing, how puberty could change people.

Amy more than anyone else. How many people hit puberty and discovered that they had superior powers? Only Amy . . . and her eleven replicas, of course.

'Earth to Tasha, come in, Tasha,' her father said.

'Sorry, I was daydreaming,' Tasha said.

'Eat your soup while it's hot,' Mr Morgan told her. 'It's delicious.'

But the soup would have to wait. A voice boomed out from the head table. 'Good evening, boys and girls, ladies and gentlemen.' Everyone turned to face Mr Drexel. 'Welcome to the third

annual National Essay Competition. It's a pleasure
to see so many intelligent and talented young
people gathered together. We're very happy that
you're here, and we hope you have a wonderful
week. I won't bore you with a long and tedious
speech now. I'll save that for later.'

He paused to allow the audience a moment to
enjoy his little joke. Then he continued. 'I know
that all you young people are nervous and excited.
But don't let anxiety ruin your opportunity to
enjoy New York. And remember, even though
only one person can win this competition, the fact
that you're here means you're all exceptional, and
that means you're all winners. Now, enjoy your
dinner.'

There was a scattering of applause, and everyone
returned to their soup. Jeanine addressed Tasha
with a particularly disgusting smirk. 'Don't be
depressed, Tasha. Maybe you'll make it to the
finals next year.'

'I didn't even enter this competition, Jeanine,'
Tasha said.

'But I thought you wanted to be a writer,'
Jeanine went on.

Tasha didn't want to lose her temper. She spoke

through clenched teeth. 'I *am* a writer. I'm a junior reporter for *The Parkside Journal*, remember? Didn't you see my article about the movie that was filmed at school?'

'No.'

Liar, Tasha thought. *Everyone* had commented on how fabulous the article was, and lots of kids had been thrilled to see their names in a real newspaper. Tasha was very proud of the article.

It hadn't been easy to write. She'd been forced to leave out the most exciting bit – how the actress playing the lead had turned out to be another Amy. An Amy clone. That was something only Tasha, Amy, and Eric knew. Tasha tried to exchange a private look with her best friend, but Amy was staring at her soup.

'Amy, your soup will get cold,' Mr Morgan noted.

'She's probably too nervous to eat,' Jeanine remarked.

This roused Amy a little. 'I'm not nervous,' she said. 'I just – I don't like this soup.'

'Really?' Tasha was surprised. 'It's good. It's got mushrooms in it, and you love mushrooms.'

'I do?' Amy said vaguely. She dipped her spoon

into the soup and took another sip. Her nose wrinkled.

Eric had almost finished his. 'Hey, if you don't want it, I'll take it.'

'Okay,' Amy murmured. But as she started to push the soup toward him, she knocked the bowl and some of it spilled out.

'Amy, your skirt!' Tasha cried out.

Amy looked down at the wet spot on her lap, but she didn't move or say anything.

'Why don't you go to the rest room and wipe it off before it stains?' Mrs Morgan suggested.

Amy started to rise. 'Excuse me . . .' She began to sway. Eric leaped out of his seat and caught her.

'Amy!' Tasha shrieked.

Eric was holding Amy up, but her eyes were closed and her head had rolled over to one side. 'Mom, Dad, I think she's fainted!' he cried out in a panic.

The Morgans rushed over. Carefully they helped Eric lower Amy to the carpeted floor. 'Amy! Amy!' Mrs Morgan called out, but there was no response. Tasha knelt on the floor next to her.

'Stand back – give her room to breathe,' Mr Morgan ordered everyone.

By now, others in the ballroom had noticed the disruption. A man ran over to them. 'I'm a doctor. What's happened?'

'I don't know, she just fainted,' Mrs Morgan said worriedly.

The doctor knelt down beside Amy. 'Does she have any allergies?'

'No,' Tasha told her. 'None.'

'Has she ever fainted before?'

Tasha shook her head fiercely. 'No, she's never sick!'

The doctor took Amy's wrist. 'Her pulse is very rapid. We need to get her to a hospital.'

'I'll call nine-one-one,' Mr Morgan said.

'Is she going to be okay?' Eric asked.

'It's probably just nerves,' Jeanine said.

Competition officials had joined them now, and the doctor was busily trying to shoo everyone away. Tasha was pushed to the side. She looked at her brother and thought she'd never seen him so pale before. He looked almost as scared as she felt.

Then the paramedics arrived and lifted Amy onto a stretcher. 'I want to go with her,' Tasha cried out.

'I'm coming, too,' Eric declared.

But Mrs Morgan took over. 'No, you all stay

here; I'll go with her,' she instructed them in a rush. To Mr Morgan she said, 'Call Amy's mother; the number's in my suitcase.' All over the ballroom, people were standing to get a look at the commotion.

Eric and Jeanine followed the stretcher out of the room, and Mr Morgan hurried off to find a telephone. Tasha didn't move. She was in a state of shock, paralysed with fear and disbelief.

Mr Drexel put his hand on her shoulder. 'Don't worry, dear,' he said comfortingly. 'People get very tense at these occasions, more than they realise. This isn't the first time a participant has passed out. I'm sure your friend will be fine.'

But of course, he didn't understand. Other people fainted, not Amy.

Amy was invincible.

5

A my lay flat on her back. She could hear a
faint, rhythmic drumbeat within the thick
glass that surrounded her. From beyond the glass,
she saw streaks of red orange. They were accompanied by a crackling sound, and she was starting to
feel warm, too warm . . . It was a fire! She was
trapped in a fire!

She woke with a gasp. There was no glass, no fire
– it had just been her old, familiar dream. The same
dream that had haunted her since she was a child
and that had recently been explained. The glass was
Amy's incubator in the lab, and the fire was the lab
explosion. Amy had been the last baby taken out,
but not before the explosion went off earlier than
planned. She had almost died. Still, she hadn't had

the dream in quite a while. What could have brought it on now?

She realised she was gazing up at a white ceiling, and she was confused. The ceiling of her bedroom was blue . . . memories edged their way into her consciousness. New York, the essay competition, the fancy hotel . . .

But this wasn't a fancy hotel room. It was a room she'd never seen before, and yet it was familiar. Everything was white, and it had a smell . . . not a bad smell, a very clean smell. Antiseptic. Like a hospital.

Then she was truly awake, and her immediate memory flooded back. Dinner, the ballroom, falling . . . She sat up. She felt a little dizzy, but not terrible. She wriggled her toes and tentatively lifted each leg. Nothing seemed to be broken. There were no tubes attached to her arms, and all body parts seemed to be functioning. Gingerly she felt her head. No bandages, no wounds.

There was a light rap on the door, and then it opened. A young, bright-eyed woman in a white pantsuit, with a stethoscope around her neck, bounced in. When she saw Amy sitting up, she smiled.

'Welcome back to the land of the living! How are you feeling?'

'Okay, I guess,' Amy said. 'What happened? How did I get here?'

'By ambulance,' the woman told her. 'You fainted at dinner last night.'

Amy was incredulous. 'I *fainted*? That's impossible, I've never fainted in my life.'

'Well, you fainted last night,' the woman repeated firmly. 'If you don't believe me, you can ask Mrs Morgan. She came with you in the ambulance.'

'Where is she?'

'Actually, she left just a few minutes ago. She was exhausted after sitting by your bed all night. I'm sure she'll be back later. Now, let's see how you're doing.'

As the woman bent over her with the stethoscope, Amy read her name tag. TAMMY RENFROE, R.N. She looked like a Tammy, Amy thought. Blond and perky. Back in Los Angeles, when her mother had been in the hospital and Amy had visited daily, the nurses had all been upbeat too. She wondered if nurses had to take classes in cheerfulness.

Tammy popped a thermometer into Amy's

mouth and then checked her pulse and her blood pressure.

'How am I?' Amy mumbled.

'Everything looks just fine,' Tammy told her with another bright smile. She removed the thermometer and studied it. 'Normal,' she said.

'Can I leave now?' Amy asked hopefully.

'The doctor needs to take a look at you first.'

Amy didn't even know what time it was. She raised a hand to look at her watch, but it was gone. 'Where's my watch?'

'It's locked up, for safekeeping, at the nurses' station,' Tammy assured her. 'We always do that with patients' valuables.' She looked at her own watch. 'It's eight in the morning. You didn't eat any dinner last night. You must be starving!'

'Not really,' Amy said. 'Well, maybe I'm a little hungry.'

'Someone will be bringing your breakfast around in a moment. Now, rest quietly, okay?' With another perky smile and a wink, the nurse left the room.

Amy sank back on the bed and tried to collect her thoughts. What could have made her faint? People fainted when they were sick, and she was never sick.

True, she wasn't Superman. If a bus hit her, *she'd* go down, not the bus. She wasn't indestructible. But her immune system was extraordinary. She thought back to the previous evening. She'd been eating soup just before . . . could she have gotten food poisoning? No. If that had been the case and something had been wrong with the soup, more people would have been sick. The way Eric had been slurping it down, he should be dead.

Well, whatever it was, Amy felt fine. And she wanted to leave. She wanted to get out of there before the doctor came.

She'd never been to a doctor in her life. There had never been any medical reason for her to go. As for her birth certificate, her vaccinations, the general checkup that was required for school registration – all those had been forged by Dr Jaleski. He had to do that for her. As her mother had once told her, Amy could never go to see a regular doctor. Any close examination might reveal her special genetic make-up.

Amy's hands went to her throat. She fingered the crescent moon hanging from her necklace and was glad the nurses hadn't taken that away with her watch. What would Dr Jaleski advise her to do now? She knew she couldn't allow the doctor here to do any tests.

It occurred to her that the nurse hadn't noticed anything unusual about her heart or her blood pressure. Apparently, she wasn't any different from normal people in that respect. Which was very interesting . . .

There was a knock on the door, but it wasn't the doctor. This time it was a girl in a pink smock, with Amy's breakfast. She didn't say a word, just placed the tray on the table by Amy's bed and left.

Amy thought the girl could do with some of Tammy's cheerful bedside manners, but she didn't dwell on it. The breakfast looked too good: scrambled eggs, bacon, cinnamon toast. The smell of cinnamon reminded Amy of the assembly they'd had back at school. That seemed so long ago now.

The food wasn't half bad, and she ate it all. She had just finished the last piece of toast when the door opened again. This time a tall woman in a white coat came in, followed by Tammy. 'Good morning,' the woman said. 'I'm Dr Markowitz. And you must be . . .' She looked at the chart in her hand. 'Amy Candler.'

'Yes, that's me,' Amy said. 'And I'm fine now.'

The doctor smiled. 'Why don't you let me be the judge of that?' She went through the same routine Tammy had performed – heart, pulse, blood pressure, temperature. Amy was barely aware of her touch. She was frantically trying to come up with some reason to avoid having any tests done.

'Well, you check out absolutely fine,' Dr Markowitz said.

Amy exhaled. 'Great. Can I go now?'

The doctor shook her head. 'We still don't know why you fainted, Amy. It's our policy to keep undiagnosed patients forty-eight hours for observation.'

'Forty-eight hours! But there's nothing wrong with me! You just said so!'

'You're right, Amy,' Dr Markowitz said soothingly. 'But it's better to be safe than sorry. I'll be by to see you later.'

Amy groaned as the doctor left. The thought of spending two days in a hospital wasn't very appealing. 'Is there a phone I can use?' she asked, climbing out of bed. 'I want to call Mrs Morgan.'

'Whoa!' Tammy said. She placed a hand on Amy's shoulder. 'Back in bed you go. I told you before, Mrs Morgan said she'd be by later with your friends.'

Amy obediently, if half-heartedly, got under the bed-covers again. Suddenly she realised she was probably a mess. 'How's my hair?' she asked.

Tammy grinned. 'If you stay put,' she said, 'I'll bring you a mirror and a hairbrush.'

When she left, Amy felt around the side of her bed and found the button that adjusted it. She fooled with it for a while, raising her legs, then her head, until she found a comfortable position. So comfortable, she felt like she could go right back to sleep . . .

In the hotel suite, Tasha watched and listened anxiously as her mother spoke on the phone. It was frustrating, only hearing one end of the conversation.

'Yes . . . yes, I see. Yes, of course, I understand,' Mrs Morgan was saying as she jotted something down on a pad. 'No, but I'm responsible for her. Her mother is out of the country at the moment, and I haven't been able to reach her. All right . . . Yes, I know the visiting hours. Thank you.'

'What's going on, what did they tell you?' Eric asked as soon as she put the phone down. 'Is Amy going to be okay?'

Mrs Morgan held up a hand as if to ward off any more questions. 'I'll tell you everything the doctor told me. She said it's not any kind of food poisoning, but they're not sure what caused Amy to faint. Maybe it was some kind of virus. The important thing is that Amy's resting comfortably now, and she doesn't appear to be in any immediate danger.'

Tasha looked at Eric. They both knew perfectly well that no ordinary virus could have any effect on Amy. But their parents were totally in the dark about Amy's superior genetic make-up, and there was no way they could be told. Eric gave a slight nod, as if he'd read Tasha's thoughts.

'What are they going to do?' Mr Morgan wanted to know.

'Well, this doctor' – Mrs Morgan checked the pad – 'Dr Markowitz, said they want to keep Amy under observation for a day or two. But we can go see her. Visiting hours are from eleven to three.' She checked her watch. 'It's eight-thirty now . . . what time would it be on that island where Nancy is staying?'

'It's just off the coast of Africa, so there's a seven-hour time difference,' Mr Morgan told her. 'It would be three-thirty in the afternoon there.'

'I'll try calling again,' Mrs Morgan said.

'Good luck.' Mr Morgan frowned. 'I've tried ten times, and I can't even get a connection. The operator said something was wrong with the lines there. I wonder if the concierge down in the lobby could be of any help. Maybe we could send a telegram.'

'Why don't you go downstairs and ask while I call?' Mrs Morgan suggested.

With her father gone and her mother busy on the phone, Tasha beckoned to Eric to join her in a corner of the room where they could talk privately.

'She *can't* be sick,' Tasha whispered.

Eric shook his head. 'She's never *been* sick. But maybe there's some special illness only clones can get, and she didn't know about it. Look, it's probably nothing. Like the doctor said, they just want to watch her and make sure she's okay before they let her go.' His tone was nonchalant and reassuring, but Tasha could see the concern in his eyes.

'What should we do?' she wondered aloud. 'Should we tell Mom and Dad what we know—'

Eric shook his head before she finished her question. 'We don't do anything right now,' he said firmly. 'Look, we're going to see Amy in two hours, and she'll tell us if there's a problem.'

Normally Tasha was annoyed when Eric took on his know-it-all, I'm-the-boss attitude. But this time she knew they were on the same side. They both understood how dangerous it could be if anyone discovered the truth about Amy. Even a doctor who only wanted to help her would undoubtedly tell the world about his discovery. And if the word got out . . . Tasha didn't even want to consider the consequences.

Mrs Morgan was hanging up after her phone-call. The frown on her face told Tasha that she hadn't received any good news.

'There's been some sort of wild weather conditions around that island,' she reported. 'Phone lines are down.'

Just then, Mr Morgan returned with the same news from the concierge. 'There's no way to contact Nancy at the moment. But hopefully the lines will be repaired within the next few hours. There's nothing we can do but wait.'

'I can't just sit around here, doing nothing,' Tasha fumed. 'And I don't want to wait two hours. I have to see Amy *now*.'

For once, her father didn't reprimand her for

being impatient. 'Why don't we go over to the hospital?' he suggested. 'Some are pretty easygoing when it comes to visiting hours.'

'All right,' Mrs Morgan agreed. 'But I think you kids should stay here.'

'No way,' Tasha and Eric said in unison.

Mrs Morgan didn't argue. 'What about Jeanine?' she asked. 'We can't just leave her.' She got up and walked out of the suite to cross the hall. Mr Morgan followed.

'Amy isn't going to want to see Jeanine,' Eric declared once he and Tasha were alone.

'And I don't want her getting near Amy,' his sister added fervently. 'I don't trust her.'

'There's nothing she can do to Amy in a hospital,' Eric pointed out.

'But maybe she's the one who put her there,' Tasha replied darkly.

Eric was taken aback. 'Are you nuts? What could Jeanine have done to her?'

'*I* don't know.' Tasha didn't have the slightest idea, but she liked blaming Jeanine. 'Maybe she put a spell on Amy?' she suggested.

'Get real,' Eric said. 'Jeanine might be a troll, but she isn't a witch.'

'That's what *you* think,' Tasha muttered.

Mrs Morgan returned. 'Jeanine's going shopping with another contestant and her mother. She wants you guys to make sure you tell Amy that she's thinking of her and hopes she gets well right away.'

'But not before the contest is over,' Tasha added.

'*Tasha*,' Mrs Morgan chided her, but at least she didn't waste time on a lecture. 'Is everyone ready?'

They debated walking to the hospital versus taking a cab. In the end they opted for a cab, but the traffic was so bad that it took almost forty minutes to arrive at the mammoth building on the east side of the city.

'Well, it's almost ten,' Mrs Morgan said. 'Surely they'll let us in to see her if it's just an hour before visiting time.'

They made their way to the reception desk and waited their turn in the short line. Apparently, this hospital wasn't too strict about visiting hours. People were giving the receptionist the names of patients, and he was telling them the room numbers.

'We're here to see Ms Amy Candler,' Mrs Morgan told the man.

The man turned to his computer screen and typed in the name. He watched the screen for a moment. Then he frowned.

Tasha was hit with a touch of alarm. 'What's wrong?' she asked.

'I don't have a Chandler listed,' he said.

'It's *Candler*,' Mrs Morgan said. 'No *h*. And I know she's here. I was with her in the emergency room last night.'

The man typed again, and his face cleared. 'Oh yes, here she is. Amy Candler.' Then he frowned again.

'Now what?' Eric asked.

'I'm afraid Ms Candler isn't allowed any visitors,' he told them.

'No visitors!' Eric went pale. 'Does that mean she could have something serious?'

Tasha let out a little cry, and Mrs Morgan took over. 'I don't understand,' she told the man. 'She's just under observation.'

'I don't have any other information,' the man explained. 'It just says no visitors.'

'What floor is she on?' Mr Morgan demanded.

The man seemed a little puzzled. 'There's no room number given, so I don't know.'

'I would like to speak with her doctor,' Mrs Morgan said firmly. 'Dr Markowitz. Now.'

The man was sympathetic. 'I'll see what I can do. Please have a seat in the waiting room.'

And so they went into the waiting room. And waited. It was a good twenty minutes before Dr Markowitz appeared. Tammy Renfroe was with her.

'I'm terribly sorry, I was with a patient,' she said. 'Let me assure you, Amy is in no immediate danger.'

'But why can't we see her?' Mrs Morgan demanded. 'I'm her guardian this week, and I haven't been allowed to see her since I brought her into Emergency last night. A little while ago you told me you were just keeping her here as a routine precaution.'

The doctor nodded. 'The fact that she's in isolation is also a precaution,' she said soothingly. 'As I told you, we have no idea why she fainted. She could have some sort of bacterial infection that might be contagious. Until we rule out this possibility, we can't allow her to have any visitors.'

'But couldn't we wear hospital masks?' Tasha pleaded. 'I saw that on *ER*.'

Dr Markowitz smiled. 'That's a television programme, dear, not real life. Now, there's nothing to
worry about. I've explained the situation to Amy,
and she understands.' She wrote a number down on
a pad. 'Here's a direct line to the station on her
ward. You can speak to me or to Nurse Renfroe at
any time, and we'll keep you posted on any change
in Amy's condition. But I don't anticipate any
problems, and I'm almost certain she'll be released
in a day or two.'

Her tone was reassuring, and Tasha's fears abated.
But she still wasn't satisfied. 'Can't I at least talk to
her on the phone?'

'We want to keep her completely tranquil,' Dr
Markowitz said. 'Really, there's nothing to worry
about. Call me this afternoon, and I'll let you know
how she's doing.' As she spoke, Dr Markowitz
ushered them towards the door. Tasha looked at
Eric. He seemed troubled too. But their parents
were nodding.

'I haven't been able to reach her mother,' Mrs
Morgan told the doctor. 'She's at a conference off
the coast of Africa, and there's been some sort of
hurricane. The phone lines are down.'

'There's no indication that we'll need to do any

64

procedures,' Dr Markowitz reassured them. 'As I told you, this is all routine; it's nothing to worry about. It's completely normal.'

The Morgan parents seemed satisfied, but Tasha wasn't. And she knew Eric couldn't be either. Because nothing to do with Amy was ever completely normal.

6

Amy wished there was a clock in the hospital room. Not knowing the time made her feel totally disorientated. And she had no idea how long she'd been sleeping.

She looked at the window. The shades were drawn, so she didn't even know if it was day or night. But she'd fallen asleep again just after breakfast, surely not that long ago.

Pushing the covers off, Amy got out of bed and started towards the window. But she didn't make it.

'What are you doing up?' Tammy scolded her as she came in carrying a little tray. 'Get right back into bed, young lady!' The sparkle in her eyes took the sting out of the scolding. Amy did as she was told, but she wasn't pleased.

'Why can't I get out of bed? I feel fine.'

'Doctor's orders,' Tammy sang out.

'What time is it?' Amy asked her.

Tammy looked at her watch. 'Twelve-thirty. Almost lunchtime.'

'Where are the Morgans? Haven't they come back to see me?'

'They came and went,' Tammy told her. 'You're not to be disturbed.'

'They were here and you didn't let me see them?'

Tammy laughed. 'You were dead to the world, sweetie.'

'When are they coming back?'

'I'm not sure. Now, don't get so upset!' Tammy smiled. 'I think I know why you're so mad about missing them. That Eric is a real cutie! Is he someone special?'

Despite her discomfort, Amy couldn't help giving the nurse a sheepish grin. 'Well, yeah, kind of.'

'I'm sure they'll be back later,' Tammy assured her. 'Now, I want you to take this pill.'

From her tray she took a small yellow tablet and a glass of water and handed them to Amy.

'What is this?' Amy asked, looking at the pill.

'Just something to relax you.'

'I don't need to relax. I'm perfectly calm.'

Tammy looked at her reprovingly. 'You don't expect me to believe that? Here you are, in a hospital, away from your family and friends. I'd be a nervous wreck if I was in your shoes!'

'Well, I'm not nervous,' Amy insisted.

'Please take the pill,' Tammy pleaded. 'For me?'

'For you?'

'If I have to tell Dr Markowitz you refused, she'll yell at me, not you!'

Amy had to smile. Tammy was sweet, if a little too cutesy for her taste. But she didn't want to take the pill. She knew enough about medicine to know that anything intended to make a person relax could also put that person to sleep. And she didn't want to miss the Morgans again.

'Okay,' she said. She moved quickly, too fast for Tammy to realise that she had dropped the pill down the neckline of her nightgown instead of into her mouth. Then she gulped down some water.

Tammy beamed. 'There's a good lunch today. I saw it coming out of the kitchen,' she confided. 'Do you like apple pie?'

'Yes,' Amy replied honestly. 'It's my favourite.' Tammy disappeared, and Amy sank back on her pillows. She certainly couldn't complain about the way she was being treated, but she was bored. And what was all this nonsense about not getting out of bed? Maybe they were just afraid she'd fall down and sue the hospital.

She had no intention of falling. She got out of bed and went to the window. Pulling the curtains open, she saw that the window was covered with bars. This didn't surprise her. After only one day in New York, she couldn't help noticing how many windows had bars on them – stores, apartments, office buildings – but usually only those on the ground floor. Here, she was pretty high up. Probably about ten floors up. Maybe New York had a lot of cat burglars, burglars who climbed down from the roof. Or maybe New Yorkers were just paranoid.

She let the curtains drop. Now what? She located the remote control for the television and sat down on the edge of the bed.

Click. It was a soap opera. She tried to watch for a minute but had no idea what was going on.

Click. A business report. Boring.

Click. A movie. Something with cowboys. Yuck.

Click. A commercial. How to lose ten pounds in ten hours. Not interested.

Click. The weather. Cloudy, with a chance of brief showers.

Click. Back to the soap opera.

That was it – five channels. No cable, so no MTV. What a crummy hospital. She fell back on the bed and stared at the ceiling.

This was ridiculous. The essay competition was the day after tomorrow. What had the .doctor told her – she'd be here forty-eight hours? But counting from when?

If her mother could see how well she was, she'd insist that the hospital release her immediately. Mrs Morgan would do the same. Unfortunately, it could be hours before the Morgans returned, and Amy couldn't stand waiting any longer. She had to get in touch with them.

She went to the door and opened it a crack. No one was in the hall, so she slipped out and moved swiftly in search of a phone.

She was lucky. She made it all the way to the nurses' station without seeing anyone, and no one was at the station, either. Ducking behind the counter, she looked around. She found a phone book and looked up the number of the hotel where the contestants were staying.

All the while, her ears were tuned to any sounds of footsteps or conversation. But she heard nothing. She took a phone off the desk and brought it down to the floor. She started to dial but quickly replaced the phone. Voices were drifting towards her. She held her breath.

She recognised Dr Markowitz's voice, and the doctor sounded testy. 'What's the problem? What's taking so long? Everything should have been ready by now.'

The soothing voice that responded was clearly Tammy's. 'I'm afraid Number Two didn't eat her breakfast. We can move the rest of them after lunch when they're all sleeping.'

Amy heard a door open, and then the sounds disappeared. But she didn't dare hang around. There had to be another phone in a more private place. She scurried down the hall and around a corner.

A public phone beckoned her. She didn't have any money, but she knew she could reach the operator without putting in a quarter.

She picked up the receiver. No dialling tone. She pressed some buttons. Nothing. She dialled 911. Still nothing.

'What are you doing there?'

Amy dropped the phone. She'd been so engrossed in trying to make her call that she hadn't heard anyone approach. It was Dr Markowitz.

'I needed to make a call,' Amy began, but the doctor wasn't listening.

'Nurse Renfroe!' she called.

In a split second Tammy appeared.

'Isn't this your patient?' the doctor demanded.

When Tammy saw Amy by the phone, her face took on an I'm-so-disappointed-in-you look.

'Oh, Amy.'

Amy replaced the phone meekly. 'Sorry,' she said. She followed Tammy back to her room.

'Do you want to get me in trouble?' Tammy scolded.

'I was just bored,' Amy said as she climbed back into bed.

Tammy picked up the remote control and turned on the TV. 'This should help,' she murmured. 'And when Mrs Morgan comes by after lunch, I'll be sure to wake you up if you're asleep.'

'I won't be asleep,' Amy assured her. 'I don't sleep *that* much.'

Tammy looked at her curiously. 'You're not feeling sleepy now?'

'No. Why?'

'Oh, no reason,' Tammy said quickly. She left the room.

Amy glanced at the television screen for a bit. Then her door opened and the girl in the pink smock appeared with a tray.

'Hi,' Amy said. 'Is that lunch?'

The girl silently set the tray down and scurried out. Amy lifted the cover. Tammy had been right – the lunch *did* look good. Hamburger, French fries, and hot apple pie. Amy wasn't all that hungry, but the pie smelled nice and tangy.

Then she caught her breath and froze.

Nice and tangy and cinnamony. She was probably imagining things. Her own mother used cinnamon in apple pies. Just because breakfast had included cinnamon toast didn't mean anything.

But she *had* fallen asleep after breakfast, which certainly wasn't a common occurrence. And why wasn't she allowed to use a phone?

And where were the Morgans? Tasha was her best friend, Eric was her boyfriend, and Mr and Mrs Morgan were practically second parents to her. They wouldn't leave her alone here for so long.

And what about the conversation she'd heard when she was hiding behind the nurses' desk? It hadn't meant anything to her, but it was strange. '. . . after lunch, when they're all sleeping . . .' When who all were sleeping? Babies? She hadn't heard any babies on this floor.

Maybe she was being paranoid. Even so, something made her get out of bed and take her tray into the bathroom. With only a tiny bit of regret, she scraped it all into the toilet and flushed it down in stages. Then she went back to bed and waited. It wasn't long before she heard footsteps coming closer. She closed her eyes and lay very still.

The door opened. She knew at least two people had come into the room. She also heard a sound she couldn't identify. It sounded like something on wheels.

'She ate the pie. It never fails. She should be out for at least two hours,' Tammy said.

'Good.' It was Dr Markowitz. 'We should have everything in place by then.'

Amy felt herself being lifted. She concentrated on keeping her breath steady and even, her eyes closed. Now she was on another flat surface and was being moved. During that time, neither Dr Markowitz nor Tammy said anything more. Then Amy felt herself being lifted again.

She was in another bed. Dr Markowitz and Tammy left the room.

Immediately Amy opened her eyes. It was pitch-black. While she waited for her eyesight to adjust, she listened for any sounds. There weren't any. At least . . .

Amy could here something – something like breathing. Someone else's breathing. And not just *one* person. More like a collective breathing.

As her eyes became used to the dark, she made out a long room with a number of beds. She counted eight, including her own. Four against one wall, four against the opposite wall. Each bed was occupied; the shapes under the blankets made that clear. The slow, even breathing also made it clear that everyone else in the room was sleeping.

Carefully, quietly, Amy swung her legs over the side of her bed and slipped down to the floor. Holding her breath and walking on tiptoe, she went to the closest bed. Straight brown hair hung down over the white sheet that covered the patient's face. She moved on to the next bed. This person, who also had straight brown hair, lay on her stomach with her face pressed into the pillow.

The person in the next bed had short brown hair, but even so Amy had an uneasy feeling. Slowly she went around to the other side to get a look at the girl's face. Her features were barely visible in the darkness, but Amy's extraordinary vision zoomed in on them.

Her breath caught. The girl's eyes were closed, but there was no mistaking the features. Amy was looking at a replica of herself. A clone.

She wasn't sure how long she stood there, staring at the sleeping girl. Eventually she pulled herself away and moved across the room to the beds on the opposite wall. Amy now knew what she would find in the beds. An Amy . . . another Amy . . . and another . . . and another . . .

Maybe it was the shock that prevented her from hearing someone come up behind her.

'You didn't eat all your dinner, Amy, did you?' Tammy asked sadly.

Before she could react, Amy felt a soft cloth on her face. And then . . .

Nothing.

7

Tasha was slumped on the sofa facing the TV in the hotel suite, but she had no idea what she was watching, and she didn't care. The TV was nothing more than background noise, a futile attempt to distract herself.

Her mother came out of the bedroom. 'Where's your brother?'

'Don't know.'

Her mother studied her for a moment. 'Where do you feel like going for dinner tonight? Your dad votes for Chinatown. I know Eric wants to try the Hard Rock Cafe. What about you?'

'I'm not hungry,' Tasha said.

Mrs Morgan ignored that. 'What about Planet Hollywood? Or maybe it's silly for us to go there.

After all, we practically *live* in Hollywood. We should go somewhere that's more typically New York.'

She was chattering, and Tasha knew that her mother was trying to distract her, but it would take a lot more than a restaurant decision to get her mind off her concerns.

'I don't want any dinner, Mom.'

'Tasha, it's not going to do Amy any good if you miss meals,' said Mrs Morgan. 'And you're not spending your week in New York moping in a hotel room. Amy wouldn't want you to do that.'

'I don't want to go out,' Tasha said stubbornly. 'What if Amy calls?'

'I just spoke to Dr Markowitz,' Mrs Morgan told her. 'Amy's resting comfortably, and there's absolutely no indication of any change in her condition. She's feeling fine.'

'I'd like to hear that from Amy herself,' Tasha muttered.

'The doctor says that if she continues to do well, she'll be released tomorrow evening.'

'She'll miss the essay competition in the morning,' Tasha said mournfully.

'And that's a shame,' her mother agreed. 'But she

can enter the competition again next year. I'm not so sure it even meant that much to her. Amy seemed much more excited about the prospect of being in New York.'

'Yeah,' Tasha said. 'And she's certainly having a wonderful time here, isn't she?'

Her mother let out a sigh. 'Don't be sarcastic, Tasha. And once Amy's out of the hospital, you'll still have time to do fun things. You can pack a lot into four days.'

The door of the suite opened and Eric ambled in. 'Where have you been?' Mrs Morgan asked.

'The library.'

Tasha looked at her brother in amazement. Her mother's reaction was identical. Libraries in general were not places that seemed to hold much fascination for Eric.

'The big public library,' Eric explained. 'On Fifth Avenue. With the stone lions in front.'

'What were you doing there?' Mrs Morgan asked. 'Not that there's anything wrong with going to a library,' she added hastily. 'I'm just – curious.'

'There was something I wanted to look up.' Eric took off his jacket and tossed it on a chair. 'About the hospital where Amy's staying.'

'What about it?' Tasha asked.

Eric looked almost embarrassed. 'I just wanted to check it out. Make sure it's, you know, legal. A real hospital.'

'Of course it's a real hospital!' Mrs Morgan declared. 'You saw it yourself. What else could it be?'

'I don't know,' he said, dropping down on the sofa. 'Maybe some sort of laboratory where they kidnap people to use as guinea pigs. I just wanted to make sure there wasn't any chance that Amy was kidnapped.'

'Kidnapped!' Now Mrs Morgan looked at her son as if she was beginning to doubt his sanity. 'Why would anyone kidnap Amy?'

Tasha and Eric looked at each other and then just as quickly looked away. 'Well, it's a dangerous city,' Eric said evasively. 'Maybe there's a gang that kidnaps tourists to − to − get body parts. To sell them for organ transplants.'

'Eric, you've been watching too much science fiction on TV,' Mrs Morgan said sternly. 'Now, go wash your hands. We're going out to dinner.' She disappeared back into her bedroom, and Tasha turned eagerly to Eric.

'What did you find out?'

'It's a regular hospital,' Eric admitted. 'The reference librarian showed me where it was listed in a bunch of medical directories. It's one of the top hospitals in the country. Famous people go there.'

'Oh.' Tasha knew she should be relieved to hear this, but she was almost disappointed. Clearly, there was nothing they could do about the situation but wait for Amy to be released.

There was a knock on the door. Tasha pulled herself off the sofa and went to open it.

'What do you want?' she asked Jeanine.

'Your mother invited me out to dinner with you all,' she replied.

'Great,' Tasha muttered, and held the door open wider. Jeanine sauntered in. 'Hi, Eric. What's the matter? You look so sad!'

All the frustration and anxiety Tasha had been keeping bottled up inside rose to the surface. 'Of course he's sad, you idiot!' she shrieked. 'His girlfriend, my best friend, is in hospital and we're worried about her! You just don't care about anyone but yourself, do you? You're probably happy about this! Now you've got a better chance to win the contest!'

Jeanine stared at Tasha openmouthed. Unfortunately, in the middle of her tirade, Tasha's mother walked into the room. 'Tasha!' she cried in horror.

Jeanine shot a quick look at Mrs Morgan and another at Tasha. Then she promptly burst into tears.

'How can you say that, Tasha?' she wept. 'I'm just as upset about Amy as you are! I didn't sleep all night. I don't even want to write the stupid essay tomorrow!' She threw herself down on a chair and sobbed.

'Oh, dear,' Mrs Morgan moaned, hurrying over to her. She stroked Jeanine's hair gently. 'I'm sure Tasha didn't mean to sound cruel. She's just so worried, she doesn't know what she's saying. Isn't that right, Tasha?'

Tasha watched the sobbing figure in the chair, and she actually felt a twinge of uncertainty. If she didn't know better, she could almost believe that Jeanine was actually grieving over Amy's illness.

Jeanine raised her tearstained face. 'Tasha, I know what you're thinking. You think I hate Amy. But that's not true! Sure, we're always competing with each other. But deep down inside, we do care about each other. And I'm worried sick about her!'

Tasha looked at her brother. 'Hey, take it easy,' he said to Jeanine gruffly. He actually seemed to be feeling sorry for the girl. With all her own doubts, Tasha had to admit she'd never seen or heard Jeanine seem so sincere. Was it possible the awful girl was changing? Maybe Amy's illness had come as such a shock she was actually going through a metamorphosis and becoming a human being. Tasha supposed she should give her the benefit of the doubt.

And now Tasha's own mother was shooting fierce looks at her. 'Tasha,' she hissed. 'Say something!'

Tasha could see that she was going to be in serious trouble if she didn't make some gesture of kindness. She considered her options. Give Jeanine a big hug and beg forgiveness? No way. She wished Amy was there. *She'd* know what to do.

Just thinking of Amy gave her an idea. She ran into their bedroom and rummaged in the top drawer of the bureau. Then she hurried back to the still-sniffling Jeanine.

'Listen, Jeanine, I'm sorry,' she said, trying very hard to be sincere. 'I guess I'm just so upset I didn't know what I was saying.'

Jeanine accepted a tissue from Mrs Morgan. 'I understand,' she said in a teeny-tiny voice. 'What's that?' she asked, her eyes on the chain dangling from Tasha's hand.

'It's Amy's necklace – the crescent moon medallion. I didn't want it to get stolen at the hospital, so I took it off her after she fainted. It's kind of a good-luck charm.' She bit her lip and considered an idea. She still felt guilty about making Jeanine cry, and she needed to make amends. 'You could wear it tomorrow, in the contest. Maybe it will bring you good luck.'

Jeanine examined the necklace. She didn't seem terribly impressed – after all, it wasn't studded with diamonds – but Mrs Morgan was looking at Tasha approvingly.

'Is it real silver?' Jeanine asked doubtfully. 'I'm allergic to nickel.'

'Oh yeah?' Tasha said. 'Me too. I'm sure it's real silver. Anyway, you'll only be wearing it tomorrow. Amy's going to want it back.'

Jeanine took the necklace gingerly, as if she was afraid it might carry an infection. But she managed a smile. 'Thanks,' she murmured in a sugary voice. 'It will help me to think of Amy while I'm writing my essay.'

'I'll fasten it for you,' Mrs Morgan offered, and Jeanine held it at her neck. 'Are you all ready to go to dinner? Let me go hurry up your father.' She disappeared back into the bedroom.

'You know,' Tasha said, 'if you're allergic to jewellery with nickel in it, all you have to do is coat the part that touches your skin with clear nail polish. Then it won't make you break out.'

'I only wear real silver and gold, Tasha,' Jeanine said. She pranced over to the mirror to have a glance at the charm hanging around her neck. 'This looks kind of cheap to me.'

She hadn't changed one bit.

The beds were numbered, one to eight. From where she lay, Amy could see the numbers on cards attached to each footboard. She couldn't see her own bed's number, but she assumed it was the same number as the one she'd found on the plastic bracelet that had been attached to her wrist while she was unconscious. Seven. The same number that had identified her in the government lab twelve years ago.

They were all waking now. Amy's eyes swept over the faces. Hairstyles varied, but that was the only thing that distinguished them from each other. Twice, now, she had encountered a sister clone. And each encounter had been a surprise, a shock. Sure there had been times when she imagined all of them – all twelve Amys – together. But even being united with seven others seemed unreal. It made her head spin and her heart fill with feelings she couldn't even name.

She watched as each girl moved to a sitting position. As they looked around, a vast array of emotions passed over their faces – shock, horror, anger, even fear.

No one said anything. Amy couldn't bring herself to speak – she kept waiting for all the Amy images to dissolve before her eyes. The stillness was unearthly.

Number Five spoke first, slowly and deliberately. 'I think . . . I always knew there was something different about me,' she said.

Number Four had drawn her knees up to her chest and had her arms wrapped around them. Her voice was soft, almost dreamy, as if she was speaking only to herself. 'When I was a little girl, I used to pretend I had a twin sister. Sometimes I'd pretend to be triplets.'

'What are eight called, anyway?' Number Six asked. 'Octuplets?'

'Something like that,' said Number Two.

Number Four gasped. 'We must have been separated at birth!'

There was another long silence, and then Number Five spoke again. 'What's your name?'

She was looking directly across the room at Number One as she spoke.

'Amy.'

Number Two looked at her in disbelief. 'That's my name!'

'Mine, too!' That was Number Three. After that, it seemed only natural to hear the same name repeated by each one.

'Amy.'

'Amy.'

'Amy.'

Number Five nodded. 'Me too. My name is Amy.'

They all looked at Amy. 'Yes, my name is also Amy,' she said.

Another silence. 'How could this be?' Number Two asked nervously. 'It can't be a coincidence. But who would give eight babies the same name?'

Number Eight spoke. 'That's not the most important question right now,' she said, her tone less fearful, more angry. 'I want to know what we're doing here.'

No one attempted an answer. 'Do you all have a birth-mark on your shoulder?' Amy-Number seven-asked. 'A crescent moon?'

'I do,' Number One said. They all did. But no one seemed to consider that any more meaningful than the fact that they had the same face. At that moment Amy realised that the rest of them had no idea who – or what – they were. Of all the Amys here, she was the only one who knew the truth. At least, *some* of the truth. Like the others, she didn't know why they'd been brought here.

And where were the other four?

The door of the room opened, and Amy Three let out a little cry. But Tammy didn't look any more frightening than she'd looked the day before. And she was just as chirpy. 'Who's hungry?' she sang out.

She was followed by the girl in the pink smock, who was pushing a long table on wheels. The table held big covered dishes, along with plates and utensils. 'I hope you don't mind serving yourselves, buffet-style,' Tammy continued. 'We thought that would be easier.'

Amy watched her in a sort of dazed amazement. From the way Tammy was speaking, she could have been a hostess at a birthday party. The other Amys stared dumbly too, except for Number Five. She jumped out of bed.

'What's going on?' she demanded, planting herself in front of Tammy. 'What are we doing here?'

'Don't worry, everything's going to be fine,' Tammy soothed her. 'Are you chilly in that thin hospital gown?'

'We want some answers!' Number Five insisted, but Tammy ignored her.

'There are slippers under your bed, and you'll find bathrobes in the closet,' she continued.

Amy Eight now leaped out of her bed and advanced towards Tammy in a threatening manner. 'Look, are you going to tell us what's happening or do I have to beat it out of you?' she demanded.

Tammy took a step backwards in alarm. Number Eight had her hands clenched, and she did look fierce enough to attack. Amy wondered if Amy Eight knew how strong she really was.

Number Five stepped in between them. 'You aren't in charge here, are you?' she asked Tammy.

Tammy shook her head. 'You need to talk to Dr Markowitz. She can explain everything.'

Number Five spoke quietly, but with authority. 'We want to see her. Now.'

Tammy had regained her composure. 'I'll see if I can find her. Eat your dinner, girls. And put on your slippers before you catch a cold.' She backoned to the girl in the pink smock, who silently followed her out of the room.

But they couldn't catch a cold, Amy thought. Didn't Tammy know that? Or was Amy the only one? She climbed out of bed and joined Amys Five and Eight. Number Five lifted a platter and revealed a tuna-noodle casserole. She sniffed.

'It smells okay,' she said.

Number Eight eyed the food with trepidation. 'Well, *I'm* not going to be the first one to try it.'

'It's not going to be poisoned,' Amy told them. 'They don't want to kill us.'

Number Eight looked at her suspiciously. 'How can you be so sure of that?'

Amy hesitated. She wasn't certain if they were

ready to hear what she knew. She came up with another reason. 'If they'd wanted to kill us, they would have done it while we were unconscious.'

The other five were getting out of their beds now and came over to examine the food. 'I'm not hungry, anyway,' Number Two murmured.

'I think I know why we're here,' Number Four said suddenly. They all turned to her. 'Like I said before, we were separated at birth. Our parents, or maybe just our mother, couldn't afford to keep us, so they put us up for adoption. Now she's rich, and she's hired that Dr Markowitz and Tammy to kidnap us and bring us all together.'

Amy was impressed. She'd never thought her own powers extended to creative storytelling. Maybe each her own superior genetic structure manifested itself in a different way.

'But why would she give us all the same name?'

Amy thought that was Number Two speaking, although now that they were out of their numbered beds, she couldn't be sure.

Number Four considered that. 'It could have been her favourite name, and since she wasn't keeping us, it wouldn't matter if we were all Amy. Or . . . or maybe she didn't name us at all, and our adoptive parents just happened to pick the same name. It's a pretty common name.'

Number Eight gave her a withering look. 'Not *that* common.'

One girl wandered over to the buffet. 'I'm hungry,' she said, and picked up a plate.

'Don't eat anything,' Amy said suddenly. 'Not yet.'

'Why not? You were the one who said the food couldn't be poisoned.' The girl hesitated. 'Weren't you?'

'Yeah, I said that, but now I have an idea,' Amy told her. 'Look, whatever we're doing here, they want something from us. And they're not rushing to tell us what, right? So I'm suggesting we do nothing until they give us some information.'

'You think we shouldn't eat?' Number Five asked.

Amy nodded. 'We'll tell them we're going on a hunger strike until they tell us what's going on.'

'But I'm hungry,' the girl by the table whined. '*You* don't have to eat if you don't want to, but that doesn't mean I have to starve too.'

'We've got to present a united front,' Amy insisted. 'We have to be on the same side. That's all we have right now.'

'How do you know they're not on our side?' Number Five remarked. 'They haven't done anything bad to us.'

'Not yet,' Number Three whispered. She started to cry.

Amy stared at Number Five. 'What are you talking about? They've kidnapped us, they knocked us out, they're holding us here against our will. That's not exactly what I call friendly.'

Number Five remained calm. 'Even so, I don't think we should do anything to anger them. Besides, if we do have to fight them, we need to keep our strength up. So I say let's eat.'

'Me too,' said Number Eight.

The girl by the table took her plate and began heaping tuna casserole on it. The others followed.

Amy was annoyed. She stepped away from the table and watched as her clones served themselves from the buffet. But one other Amy seemed to think her argument was valid. She too backed away from the table, and she came to Amy's side. Amy had no difficulty recognising this one – her face was still streaked with tears.

'You're Number Three, right? I'm Seven.'

'I think what you said is right,' Number Three

whispered. 'We should stick together. And we shouldn't do anything they tell us to do.'

'That's right,' Amy said.

The girl fiddled with a chain around her neck. 'I'm not hungry anyway. I'm too scared.'

'Don't be scared,' Amy said. 'Remember, we're all in this together.'

Number Three began to cry again. Amy put an arm around her and held her closer. It was then that she noticed what was dangling from Number Three's chain.

It was a crescent moon. Just like Amy's. A shock wave went through Amy, a shock just as profound as the one she'd felt when she woke up and saw them all.

Dr Jaleski had made *her* that crescent moon. He had told her he had no idea where the other Amys were. That he hadn't seen them since they'd been removed from the laboratory. But Number Three was wearing one of his crescent moons. And as Amy glanced at each girl's neck, she realised they all wore chains. The charms were inside their gowns. But she had no doubt what the charms were.

He'd given them all crescent moons. Which

meant that he'd known them. Which meant that he'd lied.

As Amy consoled Number Three, she knew she wouldn't be able to console herself. She had believed in Dr Jaleski; she had trusted him completely. Now she didn't know if she would ever be able to trust anyone again.

8

Watching the others eat, Amy remembered her encounters with her first two Amy clones. A French ballet company had come to Parkside to perform *The Nutcracker*, and there in the role of Marie . . . an Amy. Not long after, a horror movie had been filmed at school, and the lead had been a young actress – another Amy. Both meetings had sent Amy reeling.

But nothing could compare to this – seeing so many of her clones at one time, just a few feet away. Her sisters . . . sisters she knew nothing about. And yet it would appear that she knew more about them than they knew about themselves.

Amy wished she could tear her eyes away from them for yet another reason. She was hungry, and it wasn't easy watching them all stuff their faces. She wasn't sure when she'd last eaten. But she knew that if she was going to win their trust, she had to serve as an example to them. If she stuck to her guns, they'd have to look up to her eventually.

At least she had one Amy on her side – Number Three. The girl had stopped crying. Now she stared off into space.

Amy tried to get a conversation going. 'Where are you from?' she asked.

'Kansas,' Number Three said.

Amy's photographic memory conjured up a map of the United States. 'That's right in the middle of the country.'

Number Three nodded. 'And we live right in the middle of the state.'

'How did you get here?'

She looked at Amy blankly for a minute, and then her eyes cleared. 'Oh, you mean, here in New York? I'm on vacation with my parents and my three brothers.'

'Wow, three brothers,' Amy commented. 'I'm an only child.'

'You're lucky,' Number Three said. 'My brothers are all older than me, and they treat me like an infant.'

Which could explain Number Three's childish manner, Amy thought. 'Are you in the seventh grade?'

Amy Three shook her head. 'We have a farm, too far from any schools. My mother home schools us.'

So Number Three hadn't spent much time with kids her own age – which meant she hadn't had many opportunities to compare herself to others. Amy observed the other girls and picked up bits and pieces of their conversations. Number Two was from New Jersey. Number Eight lived right here in Brooklyn, New York. Number Four, who lived in Spain, was on a student exchange programme. Number Five, from Virginia, was on a class trip. Number One sang in a famous youth choir that was touring the United States. Number Six had come from Australia. Like Number Three, she was with her family on a vacation.

They all seemed to have arrived at the hospital under the same conditions. They'd become sick, they'd felt faint . . . and they'd awakened in this hospital.

Still, that didn't answer Amy's questions. Was it a coincidence that they were all in New York, and had the organisation simply taken advantage of the coincidence? Or had they all been brought to New York under pretence? Where were the four missing Amy clones? How long would they be kept here?

And what was going to be done to them?

Amy was almost relieved when Dr Markowitz arrived, with Tammy. The girl in the pink smock came in behind them and wheeled the buffet table away. Dr Markowitz stood in the middle of the room, a small, satisfied smile on her face. As if they'd been directed, all the girls automatically moved back to their own beds and sat on them. They were silent as, fearfully, they watched the doctor.

Dr Markowitz didn't mess around. She got right to the point.

'I know you have a lot of questions. You want to know why you're here and what's going to happen to you, and I'm going to explain it all.' She didn't have to ask for their attention. She had it, completely.

'Thirteen years ago, an experiment called Project Crescent was conducted in Washington, D.C. Genetic material was collected from humans of exceptional quality. In a controlled laboratory environment, embryos were created, cloned, and cultivated. You are the result of Project Crescent. You are not ordinary twelve-year-old girls. The people you call mother and father have no genetic relationship to you. You are identical in every way. As a group, you are exceptional.'

She paused. There was a new kind of silence in the room now, as her words began to penetrate. Amy tried to read the reactions on her 'sisters' faces. Surely some of them had suspected they weren't entirely ordinary.

The doctor continued. 'You are not monsters. You are humans of the very highest calibre. You are superior to everyone you know. You are superior to your siblings, your friends, your parents, your teachers. You are better than anyone. You can do things no one else can do.'

She gave that a moment to sink in. Now fear was fading from their faces. They were intrigued.

'We have brought you here so that we can evaluate the results of Project Crescent. In the course of the next few days, you will be observed and tested to determine the extent of your superiority over the average human being. You have nothing to fear. The doctors who will test you are all scientists from the original project. I myself was the director of Project Crescent. In a way . . .' She smiled. '*We* are your parents. We have nothing but your best interests at heart.'

She moved over to the bed labelled FIVE and sat down. 'I know you must have questions,' she said. One by one, the Amys gathered around her.

All but one.

Amy remained on her own bed. Automatically her hand went to her crescent moon pendant, and she began rubbing it while she tried to make sense out of this.

Dr Markowitz wasn't telling the complete truth, that much she knew. The doctor hadn't been the director of Project Crescent. That was Dr Jaleski's role.

Then a hint of doubt crept up on Amy. He'd lied to her about the clones. Why couldn't he have lied about his role, too? But her own mother had told her Dr Jaleski was the boss. A new, horrible doubt welled up. Could Amy even trust *her* . . . ? Nancy was supposed to be delivering a paper at a conference in Africa, but Dr Markowitz had said *all* the original scientists were here. Did that include Nancy? Was the conference just a cover?

Tammy was standing by her bed. 'Don't you have any questions to ask Dr Markowitz?'

'No.'

Tammy seemed puzzled. 'But aren't you excited? Gee, *I* would be. I don't understand you. And what was all that nonsense about going on a hunger strike?'

Amy was startled. 'How did you know—'

Tammy didn't let her finish. She clicked her teeth to make a reproving *tch-tch* sound.

'It will be much better if you cooperate, Amy.'

'Better for who?'

But Tammy just gave her a perky smile and joined the others on bed five. Amy tried not to look obvious as she let her eyes roam around the room. There had to be a bugging device somewhere. How else could Tammy have known that she'd suggested a hunger strike?

Absent-mindedly Amy continued to finger her pendant, until it occurred to her that it felt different, rougher. She examined it and noticed a dark, smudgy spot on the crescent moon. She'd seen a smudge like that before, on the inside of Tasha's bracelet, where the silver plate had worn off.

So her charm wasn't even made of real silver. That figured.

'Amy Number Seven!'

She looked up. Dr Markowitz was watching her. 'Yes?'

'You don't seem to be paying attention,' the doctor admonished her.

'I was looking at my necklace,' Amy said.

Dr Markowitz smiled. 'Do you like it? It's a little gift from us.'

Another Amy examined hers. 'I was wondering where this came from.'

'I put them on you while you were sleeping,' Tammy piped up. 'Aren't they pretty?'

Amy was truly confused. She looked at her charm again.

The group had more questions for Dr Markowitz. 'How long are we going to be here?' one girl asked.

'Just a few days,' Dr Markowitz assured her. 'As soon as we have our test results, you'll be returned to your families.'

'Are we going to be stuck in this room the whole time?' another girl wanted to know.

'No, we're fixing up a recreation area for you. After your tests today, you can hang our there.'

Another Army spoke nervously. 'These tests – do they mean we'll be getting lots of shots?'

'No, not at all,' said Dr Markowitz. She looked at the clipboard she was carrying. 'Today's tests are for vision and hearing.'

'I guess I'm first,' a girl said. 'I'm Number One.' She didn't look too thrilled by the prospect.

'We could go in reverse order,' another Amy suggested. 'I wouldn't mind going first. It's boring in here, and I want to go to the recreation room.'

'All right,' Dr Markowitz said pleasantly. 'Reverse order it will be.'

Number Eight followed Dr Markowitz and Tammy out of the room. The other girls began talking excitedly.

'I always knew I was different. I could *feel* it!'

'Kids at school are always accusing me of being a show-off.'

'I can run faster than my older brother. It drives him crazy.'

As they talked, Amy quietly unhooked her necklace and slipped it under her pillow. One of the Amys saw this.

'What are you doing?'

Amy could read the number on her bracelet. It

was Five. She put a finger to her lips and mouthed silently, '*Take off your necklace.*'

'What?' the girl asked.

Apparently, Number Five had never seen a demonstration of lip-reading. 'Take off your necklace,' Amy replied in a whisper, hoping she wasn't close enough to be picked up on anyone's pendant.

With their sensitive hearing, the others were aware of what she was saying. 'Why?' Number Five asked.

'Shhh,' Amy said, and dropped her voice even lower. 'I think the pendants are some kind of monitor, a listening device. So they can spy on us.'

'Why would they want to spy on us?' Number Six asked in a normal tone of voice. 'They're on our side. Didn't you hear Dr Markowitz?'

Amy rolled her eyes in exasperation. 'I heard her. I just don't believe her.' She didn't bother to keep her voice down now. If her suspicions were correct, it wouldn't matter now if they took off their necklaces anyway. Whoever was listening had to have heard Number Six.

Number Three started making a tentative effort to unhook her necklace, and Number Eight was looking interested. 'Why don't you believe the doctor?' she asked.

'Because she was lying to us. She wasn't the director of Project Crescent. I know, because my mother was one of the original scientists. I don't know what these people want, but you can be sure they're not on our side. They just want to use us.'

'For what?' Number Eight asked.

Amy took a deep breath. It was time for the real story. 'Everything she just told us . . . about what we are . . . I knew all this before. Project Crescent was—'

She was interrupted by Number Five. 'Why should we believe anything *you* say?'

'Because I'm one of you! We have to stick together, don't you see that?' Amy spoke in a rush. 'The real scientists destroyed Project Crescent because it was wrong. The people behind the project wanted to create a master race. They wanted to take over the world! They were evil. This Dr Markowitz, and whoever else is working with her, must be part of the organisation responsible for the project.'

Amy spoke with fervour and intensity, and she felt they'd have to hear the sincerity in her words.

Several of the clones did look like they wanted to hear more. But then Number Five jumped in.

'Wait a minute, take it easy,' Amy Five said. 'We're all pretty confused, and we don't know what's really going on, right? I mean, we've just learned something pretty shocking about ourselves! I say let's go along with what the doctors tell us to do, for now at least. When we find out what they want, then we can decide whether or not to co-operate with them. This could even be good for us, you know. We'll find out a lot more about what we are and what we can do.'

'You're wrong!' Amy exclaimed. You can't trust them!'

The door of the room opened. Tammy stood there. 'Number Seven, it's your turn.'

Amy knew they were all watching, waiting. She knew what she had to do.

She shook her head. 'No.'

'What?' Tammy asked.

'I'm not taking any tests.'

'Don't be obstinate,' Tammy chided her. 'There's nothing to be afraid of. Dr Markowitz told you the tests wouldn't hurt.'

'I don't care,' Amy said. 'I'm refusing to take any tests. Are you going to force me?'

The tension was high. Amy wished she could feel that she had the support of her sister clones. But she knew they weren't prepared to throw their loyalty behind her. Not yet.

'No one is going to be forced to do anything,' Tammy said. 'But this is a team effort, and it seems to me that you don't want to be part of it. Girls, do you want someone here with you who doesn't want to be on the team?'

'No.' That was Number Five. 'I'm sorry, Seven. But we do have to stick together, and if you can't get along . . .' Her voice trailed off. She really did sound regretful.

'Do you all agree with me that Number Seven should leave, then?' Tammy asked the others.

No one said anything, but Number One and Number Two were nodding. Amy looked at her one ally, Number Three. The girl was staring at her feet. Amy knew she wasn't going to get any show of support there.

Tammy was holding the door open. Amy walked toward it.

'Number Three, put your necklace back on,' Tammy said.

Amy turned. Number Three shot her a remorseful look. But she fastened the pendant around her neck.

Following Tammy down the hall, Amy had no idea where she was being taken. Should she make a run for it? She focused her eyes on the closed door under the EXIT sign. She could see that it was locked – and if it was made of some heavy metal, she wouldn't be able to knock it down.

She concentrated on gathering together all her wits, all her strength, and reminded herself that she was stronger than Tammy, and Dr Markowitz, and whoever else was a part of these tests.

Tammy stopped at a door. She took a key from her pocket and opened it. 'This is your room now.'

'What if I refuse to go in?' Amy asked.

Tammy sighed reproachfully. 'Honestly, you are so naughty. Of course, I can't physically force you to go inside. But your sisters back there don't want you with them. I'm sure they could get you into this room.'

She was right. Seven Amys would be stronger than one. Amy went into the room.

'Now, you let me know when you're ready to co-operate,' Tammy chanted in her singsong voice. 'Maybe your friends will be willing to take you

back. Although, the way you've been behaving, I
wouldn't count on that.'

The door was shut, and Amy heard the sound of
the lock clicking into place.

She was alone.

9

It wasn't a dungeon, exactly. More like a large cupboard or storage room. But there was nothing there, not even a chair to sit on. So this is solitary confinement, Amy thought. Suddenly she wasn't sure she had acted wisely. She couldn't unite the Amys if she was in isolation.

She wondered what Tasha was thinking, right at that moment. What had the Morgans been told about Amy? That she was sick, that she couldn't have visitors? Surely Tasha and Eric had some suspicions about this. Were they keeping those suspicions to themselves? Had they told their parents? Had they called her mother?

Amy tormented herself with these questions, creating increasingly elaborate and far-fetched scenarios as answers. A shiver ran through her. She'd seen a movie once, about a prisoner in solitary confinement. Alone, in complete sensory deprivation, he'd gone insane. Was this what they were hoping would happen to her? Could her powers protect her against madness?

Amy sat down on the floor and fought back the panic that seemed to be rising like a lump in her throat. She wasn't afraid to do battle, to run, to fight . . . but to be alone like this, in the middle of nothingness – this *was* frightening. She had to occupy herself, distract herself, do something.

A smile crept across her face. Suddenly she felt an immense gratitude to Tasha, who had made her sit through the movie *Grease* at least a dozen times over the past few years. Amy knew the movie by heart. Every scene, the dialogue, all the words to all the songs, were embedded in her memory. She could visualise every actor and every piece of clothing the characters wore. So she closed her eyes, conjured up an image of John Travolta and Olivia Newton-John, and ran the movie in her mind.

Olivia was outside in her nightgown singing 'Hopelessly Devoted to You' when Amy heard the key in the door. The girl in the pink smock came in with a tray of food. At least they weren't planning to starve her.

'What's for lunch?' Amy asked.

The girl said nothing as she placed the tray on the floor. Then she started back to the door.

'Wait!' Amy cried out. The girl didn't pause. Amy jumped up and grabbed her arm. The girl didn't put up any resistance. 'Who are you?' Amy demanded. 'Do you work here? Do you know what's going on?'

She pulled at the girl, forcing her to look up. It didn't take much effort. But one close look into the girl's face told Amy that she wasn't going to learn anything from her. She'd never seen a human being with such a blank expression in her life. The girl was like a robot. Her eyes were lifeless.

Amy pushed her aside and went to the open door. There was no one in the hall, and she felt pretty sure that this girl wouldn't pursue her if she took off. But take off where?

As it turned out, she didn't have to make that decision. Tammy came around the corner. When she saw Amy, she started making that tongue-clicking sound again. 'I'll bet you haven't touched your food,' she scolded.

The girl in the pink smock passed silently between them and went on up the hall. 'What's the matter with her?' Amy asked Tammy.

'That's none of your business, Little Miss Nosey. Go back in your room.'

Amy balked. 'I don't want to stay in there.'

'Are you ready to behave yourself?' Tammy asked. 'Are you going to start cooperating?'

'Yes.' Amy felt like a naughty five-year-old who was sorry for having caused mischief at nursery school.

Tammy played the benevolent, forgiving teacher. 'All right, dear.' She took the crescent moon pendant from her pocket. Amy didn't resist as Tammy fastened it around her neck. 'There,' Tammy said with satisfaction. 'Now you're just like the others.'

She escorted Amy back to the group bedroom. Only two Amys were still there – Number One and Number Two. They eyed Amy apprehensively as she came in.

'What did they do to you?' Number One asked.

'Nothing,' Amy said.

Number Two turned to Number One. 'See, I told you. They don't want to hurt us. I don't know about you guys, but I'm excited! Think of all the things we can do. And they can help us! Anyway, they can't hurt us.' She grinned. 'If what they're telling us is true, we're stronger than they are.'

The girl in the pink smock appeared at their bedroom door. She pointed to Number Two.

'See you guys later,' Amy Two said blithely, and walked out.

Amy Number Seven and Amy Number One sat down on beds across from each other. Number One touched her crescent moon medallion and looked at Amy questioningly. Amy shrugged. 'Maybe,' was all she allowed herself to say.

Number One looked troubled. If only Amy dared to speak honestly to her, she thought she might have an ally here. At least she could maybe make a friend. 'I heard you say you sing in a choir,' Amy said.

Number One nodded, and suddenly there was a light in her eyes. 'I love to sing. Do you sing?'

'I've never tried,' Amy admitted. 'I don't think I'm the artistic type.' She wished she could tell Number One about her recent experience, when she'd attempted to replace the actress-Amy (whose name was spelled Aimee) in a movie scene. She'd managed to get the other Amy fired.

'But we're supposed to be identical,' Number One said. 'We should all have the same talents.'

'Maybe we've got the potential,' Amy admitted. 'But I guess it has something to do with the way we've been brought-up. Are your parents artistic?'

Number One nodded. 'My father is a musician, and my mother teaches ballet. I suppose I picked up a lot from them. We're very close.' She paused. 'I always knew I was adopted. And there were other things . . . like, I always knew I had exceptional vision. In the summer, my family and I always take a long road trip somewhere, and I'm the one who has to watch for signs. It was sort of a family joke, that I could see for miles and miles. But it's not a joke, is it?'

'No,' Amy said. 'It's not a joke.'

Number One gazed at Amy pensively. 'Do you feel different now?'

'What do you mean?'

'Now that you know who . . . *what* . . . you are.'

Amy pressed her crescent moon, hoping the gesture might stop her words from being transmitted. 'I already knew. Remember? I told everyone before.'

'Oh, that's right! You're the one who said the

doctor was lying!' Number One leaned toward Amy. 'There's so much I want to ask you.'

Amy shook her head and indicated the crescent moon. Number One got the message, and her face fell. Then the girl in the pink smock appeared at their door again and pointed to Amy One.

'How can she tell us apart?' Number One asked in a low voice.

'I don't know,' Amy said. 'Maybe she can read the numbers on our bracelets.'

'But then she would have to be like us.'

Amy looked at the silent, blank-faced girl. She wasn't showing any impatience. She just stood there, still pointing.

Soon after Number One had left, the girl in the pink smock returned and pointed at Amy. Amy followed her down the hall, around a corner, and into another room.

A man in a white coat was waiting for her. 'You're Number Seven?' he asked, mumbling the words.

'Yes,' Amy said. 'What's your name?'

He mumbled something else that sounded like 'Dr Zuhzuh' and motioned for Amy to sit down in a chair.

Amy tried to sound friendly and chatty. 'Were you one of the Project Crescent scientists too?' she asked him.

He nodded. Then he turned off the lights, and a chart on the wall lit up. It was an ordinary vision chart.

Again he spoke in a way that Amy could barely make out, but she guessed he was telling her to read the letters. She did, and it was easy. Then he clicked something and another, smaller series of letters appeared. This went on until the letters were infinitesimal. Amy still had no difficulty making them out.

The hearing test seemed pretty routine too. Amy was given a headset while the man fiddled with something that looked like a fancy tape recorder. From what she could make out from the instructions, she was supposed to indicate which noise in which ear was louder.

The man began pressing buttons and turning dials on the machine. The first noises were clear and recognizable – a bell ringing, a dog barking, a drumroll. Then they became softer and more subtle. One sound was like a piece of paper being crumpled, another like footsteps made by feet clad in slippers.

Then Amy heard a noise in one ear that sounded like a bee buzzing. Actually, it was more like several bees buzzing . . . a few in one ear, more in the other. Then it sounded like a whole hive of bees. The buzzing was intense. The sound poured into both her ears, growing stronger and stronger until she felt as if she was in the hive, *with* the bees. Surrounded by bees.

Gripping the armrests of the chair, Amy tried to indicate her discomfort. But the man kept on adjusting the dials. Now she wasn't in the hive any more – the bees were in *her*. The noise was deafening.

It filled her head, it filled her body, and she was in pain. Each buzzing seemed to be accompanied by a sting. Millions of stings.

Amy wanted to tear off the headset, but she couldn't move. The noise had paralysed her. Surely the man could hear it too! But his face was impassive.

Amy tried to cry out, but the effort only shot more pain – more bee stings – through her whole being. Stop panicking, a voice within her shouted out in the midst of the turbulence. You can control this – you can decide what you want to hear.

And so Amy focused on the voice, and with fierce determination, she fought the screaming pain and struggled against the torment in her head. She couldn't erase it, but with the power of her mind she was able to muffle it, to hear the buzzing as an undercurrent, a nagging, threatening background sound, awful in its own way, but not as bad as it had been. She didn't know how long she could quell the noise before it became an over-whelming force again . . .

And then it was over. Silence, blessed silence. Power came back into her limbs.

She tore the headset off. There was a vague ringing in her ears, but she was going to be okay. She found her voice.

'What were you trying to do to me?' she yelled.

The man wasn't looking at her – he was studying some sort of printout from the machine. 'What were you doing?' she shouted again.

He didn't move; he didn't even flinch. And then it hit her, why the noise hadn't bothered him, why his speech was so hard to understand. He was deaf.

She was shaking all over – he had to be able to see that, but he didn't seem to care. Then the girl in the pink smock showed up.

121

Amy was led to the recreation area, a carpeted room with chairs and tables and a sofa. Five other Amys were there, but it was very quiet. Amy could feel their tension; she could see the echo of pain in their eyes. Clearly, they too had been put through the ordeal she'd experienced.

She made her way over to a table where Amy Number One was sitting, listlessly dragging a brush through her hair. A whole array of things had been laid out there for them: hair products, cosmetics, nail polishes. Another Amy, Number Four, was opening the lipsticks and looking at them with eyes that didn't seem to be seeing anything at all.

Glancing around, Amy didn't see Number Three or Number Five. But in all the eyes of all the Amys there, she saw fear.

This was the moment she'd been waiting for. They would listen to her now. But how could she speak, when the pendants would pick up every word she said?

Number One put the brush down and grabbed a nail file. As Amy followed her movements, something caught her eye. A bottle of clear nail polish.

She could hear her mother's words to Tasha. 'Just paint the inside of your bracelet with clear nail polish.' The polish would protect her from the nickel in the metal. It would provide a seal between the metal and Tasha's skin. There would be no contact, no connection.

Amy reached over and picked up the bottle of polish. Unscrewing the top, she made sure that the little brush was thickly covered with polish. Then she began to stroke the brush all over her crescent moon.

Number One was the first to understand what she was doing. She took the bottle and began painting her own crescent moon. Then she passed it around. The others might not have known why they were doing this, but they covered their crescent moons with polish too.

As soon as all the charms were painted, Amy decided to risk speaking. 'Do you understand now?' she asked. 'Can you see that they are not on our side?'

Two girls nodded; another one touched her head. 'The pain,' she whispered. 'I thought my head was going to explode.' Number Eight's eyes filled with tears.

Amy was full of sympathy for them. 'It must have been worse for you,' she said. 'I know a little more about using our abilities.'

'Tell us,' Number One begged. 'Tell us what we should do.'

'We're strong,' Amy said. 'Together we can overcome them. We have to if—' She stopped suddenly as the door opened.

It was Number Five. She too seemed unusually sober, though not quite as shaken as the others. She joined them at the table. 'That was pretty rough,' she said. 'How was it for you guys?'

Number One, who was standing closest to Number Five, put a finger to her lips and took Amy Five's charm in her hand. 'What are you doing?' Number Five asked, but Number One had already managed to stroke the crescent moon several times with the polish brush before Number Five pulled away.

'We think it will block the transmissions,' Amy told her. 'But we have to work fast, before they realise that they're not hearing anything. I think we'd better split up and take each one down at the same time, in teams. There are eight of us. Two should be able to overcome Dr Markowitz, but that deaf doctor was pretty big, so three need to go after him.'

'There's another doctor; I saw him pass by,' Number Eight said. 'He's not as big, but he looks strong.'

'Three for him,' Amy said. 'Okay, that takes care of all eight of us.'

'What about the girl in the pink smock?' Number One asked.

'We can't worry about her,' Amy declared. 'She doesn't seem to be able to react to anything, anyway.'

'Wait a minute,' Number Five said. 'I think you guys are jumping to the wrong conclusions.'

'What do you mean?' Number One asked. 'Didn't you just have that horrible hearing test too?'

Amy Five nodded. 'It was terrible,' she agreed. 'But I don't think it was supposed to be. Something went wrong with the equipment. Dr Markowitz is on her way here now to explain it to us.'

'How do you know that?' Amy asked, but before Number Five could answer, Dr Markowitz entered the room. Her neat hair had come loose from its bun, and she seemed upset.

'Girls, I just found out what happened. I'm so

terribly sorry.' She faced the seven pairs of identical eyes with a face deeply etched in concern. 'There was a mechanical failure in the testing equipment. Dr Zyker just discovered this when he examined the data.'

Number Two spoke dully. 'Why didn't he stop the machine when I finally managed to scream?'

'Dr Zyker is profoundly deaf,' Dr Markowitz explained. 'When he's conducting the tests, his eyes are on the readout. He couldn't have known you were in agony. He feels wretched about this. We all do.'

Should she tackle the doctor right now? Amy wondered. Would the others help her out?

'When I think of how you must have suffered . . .' Dr Markowitz took a tissue from her pocket and touched her eyes. Then she smiled. 'But do you see what this means, girls? Ordinary people would have lost their hearing completely from that experience. Weaker people might have died! But you all survived; you're all just fine. You're even stronger than we hoped you would be. We can really work together now, to channel all that power and talent you have. Girls, think of the future you'll have when you know how to use your gifts. What a life you'll lead! You can do anything, you can be anyone!'

Amy was alarmed at the way some of the girls were looking at the doctor. Were they actually buying into this garbage?

'And I swear to you, nothing will go wrong again,' Dr Markowitz said solemnly. 'There will be no more pain, no more suffering. You girls are the most precious things in the world.'

'We're not things,' Amy couldn't resist saying.

'Ah, we have a grammar expert with us,' Dr Markowitz said, her eyes gleaming. 'A future English professor! You know, each of you girls will ultimately find an area of interest that you want to specialise in. It might be in the arts, or in the sciences, or in business – but whatever you decide to do, you'll be the best in the world.'

Number Five let out a whoop. 'Amys rule!'

To Amy's dismay, two other girls echoed the cheer. Her hopes for an immediate unified attack were dashed. With three of them actually enthusiastic about Markowitz's plans, that left five . . . no, there were only seven here.

'Where's Number Three?' Amy asked.

Dr Markowitz's smile faded, and she looked sad.

'I'm afraid we had to dismiss Number Three. Something must have been defective in her genetic structure, and she doesn't have the potential that the rest of you have. There's nothing we can really do with her, so we've sent her home.'

'What other kinds of tests are we going to have to take?' someone asked the doctor.

Since Amy wasn't about to believe anything the woman told them, she didn't bother to listen. Instead, she thought about Amy Number Three.

She hadn't had time to really get to know the meek, frightened girl, but there had been something sweet about her, something that had made Amy feel protective. Amy supposed she should be happy for Number Three, happy that she was now home, safe and sound. But she'd miss her.

10

Amy was thinking, hard. What would it take to convince them that Dr Markowitz wasn't Mary Poppins, Mrs Santa Claus, and everybody's kindly old grandmother rolled into one wonderful woman?

But there were still two others who hadn't been taken in by the doctor's Academy Award performance. As the other Amys sat around the giant-screen TV with giant bowls of popcorn, Number One and Number Eight joined Amy by a window.

'At least we know the nail polish worked,' Amy commented.

Number One agreed. 'If Dr Markowitz knew what we were planning before she came in, I'm sure she would have separated us.'

Number Eight was examining the bars on the window. 'How hard do you think it would be to bend these bars?'

'Shhh,' Amy said, nodding towards the other girls. 'They've got super-hearing, too, remember. And right now, they're all so in love with Dr Markowitz, they'd probably snitch on us if they thought we were still talking about escaping.'

'What are they watching?' Number One asked.

'A video,' Number Eight told her. 'I think it's *Grease*.'

Amy winced. 'About the bars,' she said in a voice barely above a whisper. 'I think if we could get four people pulling on each one, we might be able to stretch them wide enough so we can get out.'

'And then what?' Number One wondered. 'We're high up.'

'I've got an idea,' Amy said. 'Have you ever been to a circus?'

They both stared at her as if she'd lost her mind. Amy didn't wait for a response. 'Well, if you have, you've seen acrobats. You've seen how one can hold on to another by the ankles. They can come down from heights that way, catching each other's wrists or ankles.'

Number One blanched. 'I've never even taken gymnastics.'

'It's just a question of strength and balance,' Amy assured her. 'I promise, you've got the natural ability to do this. Look down the side of the building. See how there are ledges on each window? We can hold on to those on the way down. And I swear, every girl here is strong enough to keep a grip on a ledge while six other girls are hanging from her.'

Number Eight looked doubtful.

'Listen to me,' Amy insisted. 'If circus acrobats can do it, *we* can do it.'

Number One peered out the window. 'We'd need all seven of us to reach that first ledge.'

'I know,' Amy said. 'That's why we have to talk the others into going along with us.'

'Number Five is the one they'll listen to,' Amy Eight remarked. 'She's the one we need to convince.'

Amy knew this was true. It annoyed her to see how the others looked up to Number Five. She'd expected to take that role herself – after all, she was the only one here with any experience in coping with being a clone. But she had to admit that

Number Five had a certain style, a leadership quality. Back home, she was probably a cheerleader.

Amy stared at her, trying to catch her eye. Eventually Number Five tore her attention away from the TV and looked in their direction. Amy made a gesture, beckoning her to join them.

She'd already decided to be totally up-front. They didn't agree about Dr Markowitz, but they were still sisters, in a way. Number Five was as smart as Amy was. She'd have to respect Amy's opinion.

And Amy had to try not to offend her. 'I understand how you feel about being here,' she lied. 'It's exciting to find out that you're special and to have someone like Dr Markowitz help you figure it all out.'

'No kidding,' Amy Five replied. 'I can't imagine telling my mother and father that I'm smarter, stronger, faster – that I can do anything better than they can! I don't think they'd take it too well.'

'But don't you miss them?' Number One asked.

Number Five shrugged. 'We've only been here a couple of days.'

Was that all it had been? Amy had lost all sense of time. 'But you see,' she said, 'some of us really want to go home.'

'That's so silly,' Number Five said. 'Get real! Your parents, your families, they can't help you realise your potential. They can't understand how special we are. We need Dr Markowitz if we're going to be what we want to be. What we *deserve* to be.'

'But we're only twelve years old,' Number Eight pointed out. 'Get real! We can't be the president of the United States. The queen of England. Madonna. We're not even allowed to take a job at our age!' Then she groaned. 'Oh, no, it's her again. The zombie. What does she want?'

The girl in the pink smock was at the door, and she was pointing at Number Eight.

'Maths tests, remember?' Number Five said. 'Dr Markowitz told us.'

Number Eight let out another groan. 'Don't go anywhere without me,' she instructed Amy, and left.

'You know, she's right,' Amy said to Number Five.

'We've got these abilities, but we really can't do anything with them until we're adults.'

'Dr Markowitz isn't planning to keep us here till then, is she?' Number One asked.

'How should I know?' Amy Five replied. 'I don't know anything more than the rest of you.'

'Well, some of us don't want to hang around when we could be with our families and friends,' Number One said.

'Well, some of us *do*,' Number Five snapped. 'If you want to leave, leave.'

'Oh, come on,' Amy remonstrated. 'You know she won't let us leave.'

Number Five had to acknowledge that was true. 'That's because it's for our own good to stay.'

'But we don't *want* to stay,' Amy pressed. 'And we've figured out a way to get out through the window.'

Number Five considered the prospect and shuddered.

'Yeah, you could do that, but you're not going to get me on that ledge. We're not immortal. Like I said, I think we're all better off staying here for now, and I wish we could all stick together.' She smiled sadly. 'But I guess you have to do what you think is best.'

She returned to the group watching the movie. Number One looked out the window again. 'How many of us would it take to bend the bars?' she asked.

'I don't know,' Amy said. 'Let's try it.'

'Wait!' Number One said. 'Someone's coming.'

It was the pink-smocked girl again, and she was pointing at Amy. Number Eight came in just behind her. 'No sweat,' Number Eight said to Amy. 'Fractions. It's a different doctor, a younger one.'

Amy went out into the hall. This time, instead of following, she walked alongside the girl and tried to get a conversation going. 'What's for dinner?' Amy asked her. No response. The girl didn't even acknowledge that Amy had spoken.

Was *she* deaf too, like the doctor? Amy wondered. She spoke more loudly, directly into the girl's ear. 'You like this job?' she nearly shouted.

Still nothing.

Amy jumped out in front of her, stuck her thumbs in her own ears, and flapped her fingers like a little kid. 'Nyah, nyah, nyah, nyah!'

The girl stopped. But her expression remained – expressionless. And as soon as Amy stepped aside, she began moving forward again. Amy gazed at her in wonderment.

The girl stopped again. A door was opening onto the hall, blocking her progress. And out into the hall came another girl in a pink smock. An identical girl.

Amy froze and watched the scene in disbelief. The new girl didn't seem to have any interest in *her*, and the two pink-smocked girls didn't acknowledge each other's existence. The one who was coming into the hall was letting the door swing shut.

Amy dashed forward and stuck her foot in the frame to keep the door from closing. As she watched, both girls continued down the hallway and turned a corner.

Putting a hand on the doorknob, Amy took a deep breath to steady her nerves. What was she going to see in this room – a whole row of pink-smocked zombies? She eased herself inside.

There were no other girls in pink smocks. The room looked like a doctor's office, very clean and shiny, with a sink and cabinets and medical equipment, but Amy wasn't looking at any of those things. In the centre of the room was a stretcher covered with a white sheet. Amy stared at it without moving, wishing she wasn't so absolutely sure that there was something – some*one* – underneath the sheet.

She thought she heard breathing – but no, that was only her own shallow breath. Her legs were stiff as she moved closer to the stretcher.

Yes, someone was under that sheet. She could see an arm now, hanging out. An arm with a plastic band on its wrist.

Amy knew what the band would tell her. She didn't really need confirmation. But some other need propelled her forward, to take the cold hand, turn it, and see the number on the plastic band. Number Three.

Tears burned behind her eyes, and a wave of grief poured over her. This wasn't just a girl from Kansas whom she'd met yesterday for the very first time. This was an Amy. This was her sister.

She wanted to cry, but she couldn't hang around here. She couldn't allow herself the luxury of mourning. If nothing else would convince Number. Five and the others about Dr Markowitz's real motives, this would. They were all Amys, they were all connected to each other, and they had to respond to this sight . . . to this death . . . just as she had. They had to see their dead sister.

With an effort, Amy let the stiff hand drop. Then she rushed out the door. Speed was essential – she couldn't risk being spotted. She had to get the others back here before anyone noticed that she hadn't shown up for her maths test. With her athletic ability, she could be in the recreation room in two seconds.

And she was – but that wasn't good enough. Tammy was standing just outside the door. She was wearing that I'm-so-disappointed-in-you expression.

'Were you really planning to climb out of a window?' Tammy shook her head sadly. 'Do you realise how dangerous that is? You could kill yourself!'

'Instead of waiting for you to do that for me?' Amy challenged her.

Tammy did the *tch-tch* thing. 'That's very rude, young lady. I'm afraid we'll have to put you back into isolation. It's for your own protection.'

'I don't think so,' Amy said. And she stomped on Tammy's foot – hard.

Tammy let out a scream. Amy raced past her and opened the recreation room door. 'They killed Number Three!' she shrieked. 'Come with me!'

But there was no one in the room.

11

Tammy was on the floor now, whimpering, clutching her foot, looking like a wounded animal.

'Where are they?' Amy shouted. 'Where are the other Amys?'

Tammy shook her head. 'I think you broke my foot,' she moaned. 'You nasty child!'

'Tell me where they are!' Amy insisted. 'While you've still got one good foot!' She raised her own foot threateningly.

Tammy only whimpered more loudly. Amy knew she wouldn't be able to bring herself to hurt Tammy again. What was the point? She had bigger fish to fry. She reached into Tammy's pocket and pulled out her key chain. Then she took off.

Now Tammy started screaming. Amy could still hear her as she raced around the corner. And just down at the opposite end of that hall, locking the exit door, was Dr Zyker.

But of course the screams had no impact on the deaf man. Even so, in a second, as soon as he finished locking the door, Amy would be in his line of vision, and there was nothing wrong with his sight.

And now she heard someone else, coming up behind her. She whirled around, her fists clenched defensively, ready to attack. But it was only a pink-smocked girl, and she was moving as if she'd been set on automatic pilot. She wasn't going to bother Amy. In fact . . .

Just in time, Amy ducked behind her. When Dr. Zyker looked her way, all he could see was a girl in a pink smock leading an Amy to another test. He walked past them with barely a glance.

But as soon as he turned the corner, he would see Tammy lying on the floor. And if he could read her lips, he'd be after Amy in a flash.

Amy ran ahead to the door with the EXIT sign over it. With dismay, she realised that there were at least a dozen keys hanging from the chain she'd taken from Tammy's pocket.

She looked at the lock. She looked at the keys. And then she discovered another gift – she could tell by the shape of the lock which key would fit it. It was a great revelation, since she could already hear Dr Zyker's footsteps, running after her. She got through the door and flew down the stairs.

She had just reached the first bend in the stairs when she felt a hint of a breeze. It was the impact on the air of a door opening nearby. Peering around the stairs, she caught a flash of a figure before the door closed.

She had to make a decision, fast. Go after Dr Markowitz? Or continue down the stairs and hope to find a way out of the building or some normal people who could help her?

But that could take a while – long enough for Dr Markowitz to have been alerted to her escape. Long enough to give the doctor time to move all the Amys to another location. *She* might be able to escape – but what about her sisters? She couldn't abandon them.

There was no time to think. She could hear a key in the lock on the floor above her and bolted through the door that Dr Markowitz had passed through. She caught a glimpse of another door closing at the end of that hall.

She moved quickly, hoping that Dr Zyker would assume she had continued all the way down the stairs. When she neared the door that Dr Markowitz had gone through, she realised it had a glass window, so she sank to her knees and approached it in a crawl. Pressing her ear against the door, she couldn't make out a sound. Not even any breathing.

Gingerly she lifted her head to peek through the glass window. The office must have been sound-proofed, because Dr Markowitz was definitely inside. And she wasn't alone. Along one wall of the office stood three identical girls in pink smocks. And on a chair facing the doctor was an Amy. Her plastic bracelet was visible, and Amy could see that she was Number Five.

She must be taking her maths test, Amy thought. But hadn't Number Eight told her that the test giver was a younger male doctor? This had to be a different test.

Amy couldn't hear anything, but she could see Dr Markowitz's face. It was time to put her new skill – lip-reading – into action.

She couldn't see Number Five's lips, but she saw

her gesture towards the girls in pink smocks. She must have been asking the doctor about them.

'They're what's left of an earlier experiment, a trial run, so to speak,' Dr Markowitz was saying. 'Physically, we were able to reproduce them, but the brain cells were a problem. They didn't replicate properly. They can only follow directions applied through electric impulses. There are no cognitive skills, no sensory perception. Watch.'

Dr Markowitz leaned over and pinched one of the three girls on the arm. No response.

'That's why we want to test you Amys,' the doctor continued. 'So we can figure out what we did wrong.'

Number Five must have said something, because Dr Markowitz shook her head. 'No, you won't be damaged in any way. None of you will. What happened to Number Three . . . I'm sorry about that. We didn't realise that having been raised in such a quiet environment would have made her so less capable of blocking the noise. We had no idea it would kill her. Believe me, we don't want to lose any of you Amys. You girls represent the future. We could never fulfill our goals without you. You do understand that, don't you?'

Number Five nodded, and Dr Markowitz looked satisfied. 'Now, what have you been able to find out about Number Two?' There was a pause, and the doctor began jotting something down on a pad. 'I see . . . uh–huh . . . Then she has no awareness of her athletic abilities, only her sensory ones? Interesting. What about Number Four, the one from Spain? It's remarkable that she's been able to completely lose her accent. Do you know if she speaks any other languages?' She nodded in response to whatever Amy Five was telling her and continued to make notes.

'And Number Seven. I'm concerned about her. She has a rebellious nature, and I'm afraid it may be contagious. I don't want her stirring up discontent among the others. How is she planning to escape?'

After a minute she said, 'Through a window? No, that won't do at all; she'll kill herself and whoever she talks into going with her. I just don't know what to do about her. Can't you convince her to go along? Will you try harder? Good.'

Amy was stunned. She didn't want to believe what she was learning. Amy Number Five wasn't just cooperating . . . she was collaborating! She was helping *them*. For whatever reason — and there couldn't possibly be a good one – she was betraying her sisters.

Amy felt sick and more than that, she felt sad. Number Five hadn't been her favourite, but she was a sister clone. What could Dr Markowitz have offered her to make her doublecross her own? Amy couldn't imagine a bribe large enough to make any Amy become a traitor.

Distressed and lost in thought, Amy wasn't aware of the danger. Not until both her arms had been grabbed and yanked firmly behind her.

She struggled, but the man's grip was tight. He gave a kick at the door, and Dr Markowitz looked up. She looked very agitated as she rose and opened the door. 'Where did you find her?'

'Out here in the hall, spying on you.'

When she heard the man speak, she knew it wasn't Dr Zyker. It had to be the third doctor, the one she hadn't met.

Yet something about his voice was oddly familiar. She twisted her head to get a look at him. Another shock awaited her.

'Mr Devon!'

12

No, the name is Candler, not Chandler. There's no *h*. Yes, that's right. Nancy Candler. She's with the biology conference. What? What did you say? There's some kind of static on the line. Can you repeat that?'

Tasha watched her mother straining to hear the response over the telephone. 'All right. Yes, I see. I'll try again in five hours. But if Ms Candler comes back before then, please have her call me.' She gave her name and number, hung up the phone, and looked at her watch. 'That would be midnight, our time,' she murmured.

'What did they say?' Eric asked.

'The conference people are away on an overnight camping trip,' Mrs Morgan told him. 'There's no way to contact them. They'll be back at the hotel at six in the morning.'

'Mom, can't we go to the hospital?' Tasha pleaded.

'They won't let us see Amy, honey,' Mrs Morgan replied. 'And the doctor says nothing will happen tonight. She's got a slight fever, but she's not getting any worse.'

Eric got up and paced the hotel suite. 'She's been there two days! Why can't they just cure her, for crying out loud! What kind of crummy doctors do they have here in New York?'

'They don't know what they're trying to cure,' Mrs Morgan told him. 'The doctor told me they're sure it's some kind of poison, but they can't figure out what kind. They've run a hundred tests on her, but they all come up negative. If they knew what they were dealing with, they could give her an antidote.'

'But what if they never figure out what kind of poison it is?' Tasha asked fearfully.

'Well, they're hoping it will just wear off, naturally.'

'What if it doesn't?' Eric was staring out the window. 'Could she die?'

'How can you even say that!' Tasha shrieked. 'Don't you have any feelings at all?'

The door of the suite opened and Mr Morgan came in. He too looked solemn, but he forced a smile. 'I stopped by the hospital,' he told them. 'There's no change. But no news is good news, right?' His attempt at joviality did nothing to improve Tasha's spirits. She slumped in her seat and thought about Amy.

'Did you get the basketball tickets for you and Eric?' Mrs Morgan asked her husband. 'I thought Tasha and I would go to that little French restaurant across the street. How does that sound to you, Tasha?'

Tasha just shrugged. The lump in her throat was so thick, she didn't think she'd ever be able to swallow anything again.

'I've got the tickets,' Mr Morgan said. 'But to tell the truth, I'm kind of beat tonight. You know what I'd really like to do? Order room service and watch TV.'

'That does sound nice,' Mrs Morgan admitted. 'I'm tired myself. And I want to be here if Nancy calls.'

'I hate to waste these tickets, though,' Mr Morgan said. 'They cost a bundle. Why don't you go with your brother, Tasha?'

Mrs Morgan was shocked. 'You think the kids should go alone to Madison Square Garden?'

'Why not?' Mr Morgan asked. 'Eric's fourteen; he's responsible. They can take a cab there and back. Eric, you could handle that, couldn't you?'

'Sure,' Eric said, without much enthusiasm.

Tasha had even less enthusiasm. 'I'm not the least bit interested in going to a basketball game.'

Mr Morgan looked troubled. 'Well, I don't want Eric going by himself. I suppose I could drag myself out . . .'

Mrs Morgan sat on the arm of Tasha's chair. 'Honey, you know how disappointed your brother will be if he doesn't get to see the Knicks. And your father's so exhausted.'

'How can I go to a basketball game when Amy's lying in a hospital bed?' Tasha burst out.

'It's not going to help Amy if you don't go,' her mother said. 'I think it would be good for you. It will take your mind off everything.'

Tasha scowled. A basketball game might take her brother's mind off Amy's condition, but Tasha had too much love for her best friend to be distracted by a bouncing ball and a net. On the other hand, she had no desire to stay here with her parents. Her father would keep trying to cheer her up, and her mother would fuss over her for not eating.

'Okay, okay,' she muttered. 'I'll go.' She glanced at her brother, surprised that she hadn't yet heard any objection from him. But Eric didn't seem to care.

There was a knock on the door, and Mrs Morgan answered it. 'Hello, Jeanine, come in. How was the essay contest?'

Jeanine looked even more pleased with herself than usual. 'I think I did very well,' she said. 'Of course, I won't know for sure until the winners are announced on Thursday.'

'Aren't you the least bit curious to know how Amy is doing?' Tasha asked her.

'Of course I'm curious!' Jeanine exclaimed. 'It's just that, every time I think about her . . .' She made choking sounds, as if she was going to burst into tears again.

'There's no real change,' Mrs Morgan told her. 'But she's no worse, either.'

'I suppose we have to be grateful for that,' Jeanine said. 'It's just such a shame that she had to miss the competition.'

'Oh, Jeanine, don't pretend—'

'Tasha,' Mrs Morgan said warningly. Tasha bit her tongue. But looking at Jeanine, she noticed that the girl wasn't even wearing Amy's crescent moon necklace. She probably didn't think she needed the luck it could bring her.

'There's a party tonight for all the contestants,' Jeanine told them. 'And we can bring guests. Eric, would you like to come? You too, Tasha,' she added hastily.

'We're going to a basketball game,' Eric said.

Tasha was now grateful that she'd agreed to go to the game; otherwise, her mother would have nagged her to go to the dumb party with Jeanine. Eric might not be her favourite recreational companion, but he was better than Jeanine. *Godzilla* would be a better companion than Jeanine.

'Will you be having dinner at your party?' Mrs Morgan asked her.

'Oh, I'm just going to order something up from room service before I go,' Jeanine said. 'See you later!' And she pranced out.

'Speaking of room service,' Mr Morgan said, 'I'm starving.'

'Me too,' Mrs. Morgan agreed. 'Kids, come look at the menu.'

But Eric and Tasha begged off, promising they'd eat something at the game. By the time their parents were happily settled in front of the TV with their dinner from room service, they were ready to leave.

Of course, they had to suffer through safety instructions. 'I spoke to the concierge, and he will arrange for a car to take you to Madison Square Garden and pick you up afterwards,' Mrs Morgan told them. 'Don't talk to strangers, and don't wander around the arena. Go directly to your seats and stay there. If you run into any problems, look for a police officer.'

After assuring their parents they would survive the outing, they left the room. Out in the hall, Tasha saw that the door of Jeanine's room was open. The same woman who had brought up her parents' dinner was inside, setting up Jeanine's dinner.

'Wait a minute,' Tasha said to Eric. 'I want to get Amy's necklace back.'

'Why?' Eric asked.

'Because I don't want Jeanine to have it,' Tasha said. 'And – and I want to have something of Amy's

153

with me.' She waited for her brother to make some
sort of crack. But he didn't.

'Yeah,' he said. 'Okay.'

The woman from room service was coming out
as Tasha went in. She recognised Tasha, so she
didn't say anything about her walking into the
room.

Jeanine wasn't there, though. Tasha could hear
the shower running in the bathroom. She wasn't
going to hang around and wait for Jeanine to get
out.

Quickly she looked around the room and then
went to the dresser. Nothing lay on top, so she
opened a drawer. There it was, Amy's crescent
moon necklace. Tasha snatched it up. But she didn't
close the drawer immediately. Something else
caught her eye – a plain white envelope. A scent
was coming from it.

Tasha's brow furrowed as the aroma hit her. It
wasn't a nasty smell, but it wasn't a perfume or
sachet smell, either. It smelled like something familiar.

'Eric!' Tasha called softly.

Eric came in. 'Hey, hurry up. I don't want to miss
the game.'

'Eric, smell this.'

'What.'

'That envelope. Do you recognise the smell?'

Eric sniffed. 'Yeah. It smells like—'

'Cinnamon toast,' they both said at the same time.

'Remember the assembly at school?' Tasha went on. 'The new drug that smells like cinnamon toast?'

Eric gaped. 'You think Jeanine's doing drugs?'

'No,' Tasha said grimly. 'She's too smart to hurt herself. But I bet she wouldn't mind hurting some-one else.'

Eric looked at her blankly. Then what Tasha was implying hit him. 'You think she—'

But just then Tasha heard the shower stop. She grabbed the envelope and ran out of the room. Eric was close behind. They raced down to the lobby and hopped into the car that was waiting to take them to Madison Square Garden.

Eric made no objection when Tasha told the driver to take them to the hospital instead.

Amy stared at Mr Devon in utter disbelief. The man who had popped up in her life in different roles – as an assistant principal, as a make-up artist – was here again. She'd never been sure whose side he was really on, but each time before, he had helped her. Only, what was he up to this time?

She got the answer right away.

'This is Dr Franklin, Amy,' Dr Markowitz said. 'He's a member of the project too. What were you doing in the hall, Amy? Why aren't you with the others?'

Mr Devon, or Dr Franklin, or whoever he was, answered. 'She's supposed to be with me, taking her maths test. I'll take her to my office.'

'All right,' Dr Markowitz said, but Amy wasn't so sure. Was Devon here to save her? Or was he a part of this organisation?

She wasn't about to risk learning the truth now. Not when she had an open window, unbarred, just three feet away. With a violent effort, she broke free of Devon's grip and leaped across the room.

'Stop her!' Dr Markowitz cried out. Number Five attempted to block Amy's progress. But Amy had more experience using her abilities than Number Five did. She was able to kick the other clone aside. Less than a second later, she was balancing on a window ledge.

She could hear Dr Markowitz shouting at her.

'Stop where you are! You're going to kill yourself!' Meanwhile, she found a brick that protruded from the wall and gripped it tightly.

Trying to figure out her next move, Amy let her eyes drift downwards, and her head began to spin. She thought she might throw up. Heights had never bothered her before – but then, she'd never experienced heights while hanging from a brick.

A *loose* brick. She could feel it coming out of the mortar.

As she slipped, she heard a scream. She wasn't sure if it was coming from her or from someone inside the office. But she didn't drop far. Now she was hanging from the ledge.

She looked up. She could see them – Dr Markowitz, Amy Number Five, and Devon. Dr Markowitz was clearly distraught. Number Five looked unnerved. Only Devon was completely impassive.

Dr Markowitz reached out the window, grabbed her wrist, and tugged. But Amy's grip on the ledge held firm.

'Number Five, you're stronger than I am,' Dr Markowitz yelled. 'Pull her in!'

Number Five did as she was told. She clutched Amy's other wrist. Now Amy could feel a slight pull. 'I can't do it on my own!' Number Five cried out.

Amy heard Devon's voice. 'I'll get the others. They can form a chain.'

Amy looked down. The next ledge couldn't be far away. Then a wave of nausea hit her.

There were no more windows on this side of the building. No more ledges. The wall was flat brick, all the way down. Nothing to grab on to at all.

Number Five spoke to her. 'You're crazy, you know that? Don't you understand anything? We could rule the world!'

'You're playing right into their hands,' Amy warned her. '*They* want to rule the world! They're just using us!'

'So what?' Number Five leaned closer. 'We're stronger, we're smarter.' She took a quick look over her shoulder and dropped her voice to a whisper. 'If they get out of hand, we'll make them disappear! Think about it, Amy! We can get rid of anyone we don't want!'

'No one should have that kind of power!' Amy shot back. 'Not them, not us!' She felt Number Five's hold on her wrist tighten.

'Don't be an idiot! We're on the same side!' Number Five hissed.

She could hear Dr Markowitz fretting behind Number Five. 'Where is Franklin with the other Amys?'

'I'm *not* on your side, Number Five,' Amy declared. 'I'll fight you just like I'll fight them!'

Number Five's eyes narrowed. 'You know, Number Seven . . . you're a real pain. She released her hold on Amy's wrist. But the relief was only momentary.

Because Number Five used her newfound strength to push Amy's hands off the ledge.

13

It wasn't so bad, falling. She felt like she'd broken free, like she had truly been released from prison. And she wasn't afraid, not really. Especially when she realised that Mr Devon was down below, waiting to catch her . . . but how could that be?

'Amy . . . Amy . . .'

They were still calling her, Dr Markowitz, Number Five, all the Amys . . .

'Amy . . . Amy . . .'

She tried to concentrate. It wasn't a girl's voice, it was a boy's voice, and it was a voice from the past . . . Eric?

'Mom, look, I think she's opening her eyes!'

It *was* Eric. And Tasha . . . and Mr and Mrs Morgan . . . and a nurse she'd never seen before.

'What happened?' Amy asked. 'Where am I?' Her vision began to clear, and she recognised the hospital room. She'd been here before . . .

She struggled to sit up. 'Hey, take it easy,' Eric said. 'You've been sick.'

'I have?'

'It was Jeanine,' Tasha said. 'She poisoned you with that new drug, the stuff that smells like cinnamon toast.'

'Now, Tasha,' Mrs Morgan said, 'you don't really have any proof of that.'

'Mom, we found the drug in her drawer!' Eric said. He took Amy's hand. 'We brought it over here so the doctors could analyse it. Once they did, they were able to counteract its effects.'

'Well, Jeanine says the drug was given to her by another essay contestant,' Mrs Morgan said. 'And Jeanine was planning to give it to the officials so the contestant could be eliminated from competition.'

The nurse spoke. 'You were never in any real danger, Amy. But we couldn't let you go until we knew what was causing the fainting spells.'

'Spells?' Amy asked. 'More than one?'

'The doctor told us you were going in and out of consciousness,' Mrs Morgan said.

'But you'll be fine now,' the nurse assured her. 'In fact, if you feel strong enough, you can leave today. The doctor's already signed your release.' She indicated the paper she was holding.

'What doctor?'

'Dr Markowitz, of course,' the nurse said.

'She's been treating you since you were admitted,' Mrs Morgan told her. 'She's been very nice, keeping us informed.'

The door opened.

'Here comes your lunch,' Tasha said. 'Yuck, it doesn't look very appetising.'

Amy wasn't looking at the food. She was looking at the girl in the pink smock who was carrying it. When the girl was close enough to her bed, she reached out and pinched her arm.

'Ow!' The girl drew back and looked at her in alarm.

'I'm sorry,' Amy said. 'I don't know why I did that.'

'You're probably still a little out of it,' Tasha said.

'Do you feel strong enough to leave, Amy?' Mr. Morgan asked worriedly.

'Absolutely,' Amy said. She swung her legs over the side of the bed.

The nurse helped her stand up. 'I've got your clothes right here.'

'We'll wait for your outside,' Mrs Morgan said. 'Come on, everyone.'

The nurse brought her clothes to her, and Amy dressed herself. 'There was another nurse here, when I first came,' she said casually. 'Her name was Tammy. Do you know her?'

'Oh, sure, I know Tammy,' the nurse said. 'She's not in today. Poor girl, she broke her foot.'

'Really?' Amy murmured. But it was just a dream, she thought. A hallucination from the drug, that was all. Tammy's broken foot . . . it was just a coincidence.

At least, that was what she had to believe. For now.

She left the hospital room to find her wonderful, ordinary friends waiting to take her back to her wonderful and not-so-ordinary life.

Memo from the Director

THE ORIGINAL SUBJECT UNDER OBSERVATION IS
PROVING TO BE DIFFICULT AND UNRESPONSIVE. IF
SHE IS TO BE INCLUDED IN THE STUDY, SPECIAL
CONSIDERATIONS WILL HAVE TO BE MADE.

Collect the Replica series!

Book 1: Amy, Number 7

Amy Candler knows she's different. In fact, she's not Just different, she's perfect!

Suddenly she can and hear things over huge distances. She can perform somersaults like an Olympic gymnast. And she knows the answer to *every* question her teachers ask!

But there's one question Amy can't answer. Why is her past so mysterious? Why can't she find out where she was born? All Amy knows is that her recurring nightmare seems to be telling her something, and that a crescent-shaped birthmark on her back has only just appeared there . . . And weirder still, someone is sending her anonymous warnings to keep her 'special' talents a secret.

Slowly Amy is piecing together her identity – but she'd better hurry – time is running out . . .

HODDER

Also by Hodder Children's Books

Collect the Replica series!

Book 2: Pursuing Amy

Amy Candler knows she's different. In fact, she's not Just different, she's perfect!

Now that Amy has discovered exactly who she is – she needs some more answers, and she needs to share her thoughts with somebody. Not being able to talk to her best friend, Tasha, doesn't help – and now that her mum has a new boyfriend, Amy doesn't want to worry her . . .

But as soon as Amy finds the one person who really understands, she puts his life in danger. And from that point on Amy feels she can't turst anybody – even the people close to her . . .

If only Amy hadn't ignored the warnings not to be perfect . . . .

h HODDER

Also by Hodder Children's Books

Collect the Replica series!

Book 3: Another Amy

Amy Candler knows she's different. In fact, she's not Just different, she's perfect!

Just as she's starting to get used to her strange life, Amy bumps into another Amy – a girl who is identical to her. Amy is scared but excited – maybe they could be friends?

But although they look the same, their personalities are totally different. The other Amy is a spoilt show off – determined to stand out from the crowd – she can't stand the thought that she has a clone.

And this girl will stop at nothing to get her way . . .

REPLICA
Marilyn Kaye

0 340 74951 2	Amy, Number 7	£3.99	☐
0 340 74952 0	Pursuing Amy	£3.99	☐
0 340 74953 9	Another Amy	£3.99	☐

All Hodder Children's books are available at your local bookshop, or can be ordered direct from the publisher. Just tick the titles you would like and complete the details below. Prices and availability are subject to change without prior notice.

Please enclose a cheque or postal order made payable to *Bookpoint Ltd*, and send to: Hodder Children's Books, 39 Milton Park, Abingdon, OXON OX14 4TD, UK. Email Address: orders@bookpoint.co.uk

If you would prefer to pay by credit card, our call centre team would be delighted to take you order by telephone. Our direct line *01235 400414* (lines open 9.00 am–6.00 pm Monday to Saturday, 24 hour message answering service). Alternatively you can send a fax on *01235 400454*.

TITLE		FIRST NAME		SURNAME	

ADDRESS	
DAYTIME TEL:	POST CODE

If you would prefer to pay by credit card, please complete:
Please debit my Visa/Access/Diner's Card/American Express (delete as applicable) card no:

Signature . . . . Expiry Date . . . .

If you would NOT like to receive further information on our products please tick the box. ☐